Maggie

Maggie

Marion Chesney

Thorndike Press • Chivers Press
Waterville, Maine USA Bath, England

This Large Print edition is published by Thorndike Press, USA and by Chivers Press, England.

Published in 2002 in the U.S. by arrangement with Lowenstein Associates, Inc.

Published in 2002 in the U.K. by arrangement with the author.

U.S. Hardcover 0-7862-3623-X (Candlelight Series)
U.K. Hardcover 0-7540-4967-1 (Chivers Large Print)
U.K. Softcover 0-7540-4968-X (Camden Large Print)

The text of this Large Print edition is unabridged.
Other aspects of the book may vary from the original edition.

Cover design by Thorndike Press Staff.

Set in 16 pt. Plantin by Christina S. Huff.

Printed in the United States on permanent paper.

British Library Cataloguing-in-Publication Data available

Library of Congress Cataloging-in-Publication Data

Chesney, Marion.
    Maggie / Marion Chesney.
      p. cm.
    ISBN 0-7862-3623-X (lg. print : hc : alk. paper)
    1. Large type books. I. Title.
  PR6053.H4535 M3 2002
    823´.914—dc21   2001053425

For Iain Mackay and his sister,
Mrs. Barbara Macleod . . .
the best holiday-makers in Beauly.

One

Thin curtains of rain swept over the low hills of the Black Isle towards the shallow waters of the Beauly Firth. A great gust of damp wind struck against Maggie Fraser's cheek as she hurried homeward. The silver birch trees on her left tossed and swayed as the wind whistled through them. With a great roar like some beast heading for its lair, the wind hurtled across the road and dived into the dark, green, piney depths of the deer forest on her right. All was silent again.

A yellow shaft of sunlight struck through the clouds and shone down on the curve of the road ahead, illuminating the white walls of Maggie's father's shop. And then the trailing curtains of rain hid it from sight.

Maggie quickened her step. She must reach home before her father, or he would demand to know where she had been. And if he found she had been wasting the afternoon at the library in Beauly she would receive a beating, for Mr. John Fraser had an unhealthy disrespect for education.

Although Fraser was a local name and John Fraser had implied he was returning to the area of his birth to set up shop, no one could remember him as a boy. It was known he had come from Skye twelve years ago where he had been crofting. It was known his wife was dead and that he treated his daughter, Maggie, disgracefully. But very little else was known about him and certainly nothing was known about his origins. He had opened up a grocery store by converting a small croft about halfway between Beauly and Inverness. The shop stood at a bend on the road which ran between Beauly and Inverness, but everyone prophesied failure. For who would travel miles from Beauly, already well-served with shops, to buy their groceries? And it was unthinkable that anyone would be mad enough to travel from Inverness to shop at a dingy little store which did not even carry any speciality goods.

But John Fraser had prospered. He not only sold his goods cheaper than anywhere else, but he catered to the great hordes of cyclists who descended on the Highlands of Scotland every summer. Cycling was all the rage and cyclists always seemed to want to buy groceries as soon as they were out of sight of the nearest town.

Education was something sinister and

strange to John Fraser. He had made sure that Maggie spent only long enough at school to be able to keep the shop accounts, and so, as soon as she could write with a fair hand and add up columns of figures, he had promptly put an end to her schooling when she was twelve years old.

Maggie was now eighteen and despite six years of drudgery and ill-treatment, she had grown into a real Highland beauty with jet-black hair and large brown eyes flecked with gold like peaty Highland pools shining in the sun. Her skin was very white and fine and she had a good figure, although it was not often visible because of the layers of old clothes she wore to keep herself warm.

There had been various attempts to knock some sense into John Fraser's head with regard to Maggie's education. But no one really tried very hard because John Fraser could be quite frightening, and, anyway, Maggie was only a girl, and everyone knew education was wasted on mere girls whose sole function in life was to marry and beget children.

Maggie pulled her shawl over her head as the rain poured down. How long the road seemed! The one afternoon a week when the shop closed early was her only time of freedom. Her father went off somewhere every Wednesday afternoon, returning late and drunk. Maggie never knew where he went and she could not imagine him at some inn, propping up the bar amid the cheerful clatter of glasses and conversation of the local people, for he was a withdrawn, angry man.

Mrs. Fraser had died when Maggie was eight and when the Frasers were still living on the Isle of Skye. Maggie remembered her as a bitter woman with a red nose and pale grey eyes, with a thin body wrapped in an old tartan shawl.

One day she had been found dead of a heart attack and Maggie had spent long, miserable days and nights tortured with guilt. For she had found she could not feel one bit of sorrow or loss. It was shortly after his wife's death that John Fraser had announced they were moving to the mainland. Where he got the money from was a mystery. But Maggie was allowed to wear shoes for the first time in her life. The excitement of the journey was soon dimmed by her father's hectoring bad temper. Without Mrs. Fraser as a butt, Maggie had realized gloomily, she would now have to bear the full brunt of her father's spleenish bad temper.

The shop was finally reached. Maggie took the heavy iron key which she kept tied on a string around her waist and cautiously opened the door.

Silence.

She heaved a sigh of relief. The shop was dim and smelled of pepper and bacon and cheese. Pale yellow light came in through the thin blind over the shop door.

Maggie went into the small kitchen at the back of the shop, opened the iron lid of the stove and threw in some pine cones and torn newspapers and lit the fire. The rain, heavy now, drummed on the tin roof of the kitchen which was a makeshift extension to the small building.

She pushed open the back door and leaned against the jamb. There was no garden to speak of, only a scrubby area of wild lupins, broom, tussocky grass and old cardboard boxes.

Maggie remembered the book she had been reading that afternoon. She did not borrow books from the library and take them home, knowing her father would burn them, but rather contented herself with a half day a week's orgy of reading.

Although Maggie still thought in Gaelic, she had learned to read and speak English very well, her voice soft and lilting.

The story Maggie had been reading that afternoon had been about a poor girl who had been courted by a handsome lord. But she had spurned his advances in favour of those of her country swain. It had all been very disappointing because Maggie had quite fallen in love with the handsome lord who was a terrible rake, but he had been killed in the Boer War, atoning his sins by dying for Queen and Country.

Suddenly all the fear of what her father would be like on his return struck her, and she began to shiver. When she was much younger, Maggie had firmly believed in the fairies and had left little gifts of milk and oatcakes for them, creeping out in the middle of the night when her father was asleep, and laying her small offerings by the kitchen door, and silently begging the wee folk to take her father away. But the next day, the oatcakes and milk would be gone but John Fraser would be very much present. It was only when Maggie found a very fat hedgehog wandering away from the empty milk saucer one morning that she realized it had not been the fairies who had been enjoying her gifts.

She returned to the kitchen and put a couple of logs on the fire and, taking the lid off the top of the stove, swung the heavy griddle which served as a frying-pan over the flames. Her father liked fried food and Maggie knew that if she could get him to eat immediately after he arrived, he would soon pass out. She fried slices of black pudding and white pudding, two rashers of bacon, a slice of dumpling and a slice of haggis. It could all be reheated quickly if her father arrived late.

The bell above the shop door clanged and her heart leapt into her mouth.

John Fraser came lurching into the kitchen. He was a tall, stooped, thin, gangling man with a lantern-jawed face and very pale blue eyes under shaggy eyebrows.

"Whit's this?" he demanded. "Are ye wastin' my food?"

"It's for you, Father," said Maggie, reaching for an egg.

"Oh, it is, is it?" he sneered. "Weel, afore ye dae anything else, jist gang ben the shop and bring me a dram."

Maggie's heart sank. If he had eaten right away, then she would have been safe. But a dram before the meal always led to another and another and then a beating. Also, he was speaking English which was a very bad sign. Mr. Fraser spoke English only to 'the tourists' as he called anyone who came from a distance of more than twenty miles. The only other time he spoke English was when he was about to take off his leather belt and beat his daughter.

13

Maggie went into the shop to search under the counter which was where the bottle of whisky was kept. While she was bending under the counter, her eye fell on a cardboard box full of small bottles which had obviously just arrived that day. On the outside of the box it said 'Dr. Simpson's Sleeping Draught'.

Maggie looked from the half-empty whisky bottle to the bottle of sleeping medicine and her heart began to hammer against her ribs.

"What's keepin' ye?" yelled her father. "A taste o' the belt is what you need to cure your lazy ways."

Maggie ceased to think. She picked up the bottle of sleeping draught, pulled the small cork out with her teeth and tipped a large measure into a glass and then topped the glass up with whisky. Somewhere outside the walls of bone-like numbness that pressed on her brain, her conscience was clamouring to get in. She carried the glass in very carefully and set it on the table.

He picked up the glass and raised it to the light. "Now, what did ye do with yersel' today?" he asked, his voice soft with menace.

Maggie stared at him, her white face even whiter, glowing luminous in the dark, firelit kitchen. Her mother had read the Bible to her every night and Maggie had learnt all about the fear of God, Mrs. Fraser being very fond of the gorier parts of the Old Testament. She knew if she lied, then the wrath of God would be terrible indeed.

"I . . ." began Maggie miserably when there came a pounding at the shop door.

"Go and see who that iss," snapped Mr. Fraser, his Highland accent made doubly sibilant by the amount of whisky he had consumed. "Serve them what they want. But keep the blind down or we will haff some of they jealous shopkeepers from Beauly complaining about me opening on the half day."

Glad of the small reprieve, Maggie went quickly into the shop and opened the door.

The man who stood there seemed to fill the doorway. Behind him in the rain stood a horse and gig.

"Yes, sir?" asked Maggie.

The man did not reply but stood looking at her. He was thick-set with a large beefy face and a thick black moustache. He wore a hard bowler hat and an Inverness cape over a blue worsted suit. His eyes were small and black. They roamed over Maggie's body in a way that made her pull her shawl more tightly about her shoulders.

"Yes, sir?" demanded Maggie again, her

voice sharpened with fright. For the full enormity of what she had done finally hit her and all she wanted to do was to run back into the kitchen and snatch the glass from her father's hand.

"I would like two ounces of black tobacco," said the man, stepping into the shop and removing his bowler to reveal a thick head of brown hair well-oiled with bear grease.

"Certainly," said Maggie breathlessly.

"It's bad weather in these parts," said the man, leaning against the counter. "I am from Glasgow."

"Yes," said Maggie faintly, trembling fingers measuring out the tobacco.

"Aye, I am an Inspector of Police." Maggie dropped the tobacco on the floor and stared at him wild-eyed as if he had somehow, by diabolical means, divined her crime and was now playing with her as a cat plays with a mouse.

"Now whit have ah said to frichten a beauty like you?" he grinned, offering a hand which Maggie shook. His hand was like a fat, damp cushion.

"My name is Macleod," the customer went on. "Inspector James Macleod."

There was a terrible crash from the kitchen and Maggie let out a squeak of pure terror.

Mr. Macleod looked at her sharply and then walked into the kitchen with Maggie hurrying after him.

Mr. Fraser lay on the kitchen floor, snoring stentoriously. The glass which had held his whisky — and sleeping potion — lay unbroken on the floor beside him.

Mr. Macleod looked from the glass to the bottle on the table and then leaned forward and sniffed.

"Drunk," he said, straightening up. "Dead drunk."

"Oh, please, sir," begged Maggie, "if I can just give you your tobacco . . ."

"Nonsense. I'll get him to his bed. Your faither? Aye, ah thought so. Where does he sleep?"

Maggie pushed open the door of a small bedroom which led off the kitchen. The inspector took Mr. Fraser under the shoulders and dragged him into the bedroom and hefted him onto the bed.

"He'll sleep it off," he grinned. "Well, lassie, let's hae that tobacco."

Maggie flew into the shop, desperately anxious to get rid of him.

She measured out the tobacco and rolled it up in a twist of paper.

Mr. Macleod patted his pockets. "I've no small change," he said. "Tell you what, I'm only going as far as Muir of Ord. I'll be back the morn's morn, and I'll pay ye then."

"That will be all right," said Maggie, while inside her head a voice screamed, "Go!"

There was something furtive and sly about the big inspector. His little black eyes took a final promenade over her body and then to Maggie's infinite relief, he left, cramming his bowler hat down on his head.

She shut and locked the shop door after him and went slowly into her father's bedroom.

Mr. Fraser lay snoring with his mouth open. The small room smelled strongly of spirits.

"What if he dies?" thought Maggie, "and me with an inspector of the Glasgow police to witness I was the only person here!"

She went back into the shop and carefully read the label on the now two-thirds full bottle of sleeping potion. It did not list the ingredients, only quotes from letters from eminent people who claimed to have been soothed and refreshed by it. "This mixture is tasteless," she read. Goodness! She had never even thought of that.

There was nothing she could do now but fill up the bottle with water so that her father would not notice the missing liquid and then pray he would not die. She wanted him to die and had often longed for his death. But she could not think of living with such a weight of guilt.

After some time, she reheated the meal she had prepared for her father and ate it. With luck, he would remember nothing. If she left the food uneaten, then he would beat her for wasting it.

Feeling calmer after she had eaten, Maggie took another look at her father. He had rolled on his side and was sleeping peacefully. The fear began to leave her heart.

The inspector would not return. He had seemed a sly, cunning sort of man and was no doubt in the habit of cheating small shopkeepers. And tomorrow would not be so bad provided she said nothing to annoy her father.

Her father was only tolerable the day after one of his drinking bouts when he was consumed by guilt. Maggie decided to say nothing about the inspector.

She was so very sure he would not be back.

The small shop was busy the next day. Pale and wan, John Fraser shambled about behind the counter, darting furtive looks at his daughter as she sliced bacon and cut cheese and measured lentils and dried peas and sugar into paper bags. He was wondering how on earth she had managed to get

19

him to bed. Or had he gone to bed himself? But, he had woken with all his clothes on, and his boots as well.

Maggie worked away efficiently. The wrath of God would soon fall on her head, that she knew. For one could not do so dreadful a thing as drug one's father's whisky and escape Scot free. If His eye was on the sparrow, it was most certainly fixed on one small sinner with a bottle of sleeping potion in her hand.

She could only make up her mind to accept her punishment stoically when it came. In the meantime, she could only be glad that the inspector had not put in an appearance.

But, all of a sudden, he was there, leaning up against the counter and grinning with lecherous familiarity. He paid for the tobacco and Maggie took the money in her small hand and waited for her father to spring forward and demand to know what it was all about. But for once, John Fraser stayed in the corner of the shop, listening.

The inspector questioned Maggie jovially about her age, her life and her friends. Maggie patiently answered all of his questions, waiting for her father to interrupt as he always did when some of the male customers seemed to become too interested. But still her father stayed away, pretending to count tins of groceries in the corner.

The inspector then bragged about his big house in Glasgow and how he expected to be made superintendent one day soon. "Aye, it's a fine big house, I have," boasted the inspector, "right out in the West End, the best part o' the town. It needs a mistress though . . ." He suddenly grinned slyly at John Fraser and laid a finger alongside his nose.

John Fraser came forward at last, cracking the knuckles of his long, bony, red hands.

"I jalouse your frae the big city, sir," said Mr. Fraser. "Perhaps you would care tae step into the back shop and hae a drap o' the cratur to warm ye?"

The inspector grinned again, and his grin was reflected on John Fraser's face as if both men had come to some telepathic understanding.

Maggie watched them go in amazement. It was unheard of for her father to offer anyone hospitality.

She served the other customers and then closed and locked the shop. Occasionally the voices from the kitchen would rise and she could hear, at one point, her father protesting, "No, I wad not take that sort of money for a cow let alone for ma ain . . ."

and then his voice dropped and the rest of the words were lost.

Maggie waited and waited, but still the murmur of voices rose and fell.

At last, she opened the shop door again and slipped outside. The road curved one way to Beauly, the other to Inverness. The evening was calm and still with great shafts of yellow sunlight shining down on the deer forest on the other side of the road. A clump of foxgloves glowed in the clear light and clumps of blue harebells trembled at the edge of the ribbon of road.

There was the cracking of a twig and Maggie looked up. A doe stood at the edge of the trees across the road.

"Maggie!" sounded John Fraser's voice from the back of the shop.

The doe and Maggie looked at each other with wide frightened eyes. Then the doe turned and fled into the dark green gloom of the forest and Maggie walked back into the shop and shut the door and locked it.

Squaring her shoulders, she walked into the kitchen. To her surprise her father did not seem to have had very much to drink. The inspector had been drinking heavily, for his red face was even redder and little beads of sweat stood out on his brow above his black, glittering eyes.

"Aye, there's my girl," said Mr. Fraser, putting a bony arm about Maggie's shoulders. "Weel, Maggie, ye cannae say I don't do ma best for ye.

"You're to be married to Mr. James Macleod."

Two

The Earl of Strathairn looked out of the window of his carriage and shivered. "It looks like hell," he said, and his Highland manservant, Roshie Munro, leaned forward and arranged the thick carriage rugs around his master's knees.

"Weel, my lord," he said, "Glasgow was aye like this."

The earl shivered again. Thick, yellow, acrid fog swirled around the streets, thinning slightly at the corners to show vistas of looming black tenements with their cavernous closes, or communal passageways, lit by flaring jets of gas. Incredibly filthy shawled women loomed up out of the fog, their scabby faces and dropsical bodies looking like something out of the illustrations of Hogarth. A drunk, red-eyed and wild, peered in the window as the carriage halted in the press of traffic and the earl turned his head away and longed for the blue skies and heat of India.

India. It seemed that only a short time ago

that country had been his future, and his only worries his mess bills.

He had been captain in a sepoy regiment on the North-West Frontier. His parents, a scholarly couple, were dead, leaving him only a small annuity from their meagre estate near Oxford. He was thirty-two and unmarried, since he felt he could not afford the added expense of a wife. He had never been in love. He had had many opportunities to wed quite wealthy girls but had found himself drawn to none of them and would not marry for money. Besides, most of the girls who were shipped out to India were the ones who had failed to 'take' during several London Seasons and were not noted for their looks. He had once toyed with the idea of paying serious court to a very beautiful Indian girl, but her family was of a very high caste indeed, and wished to do better for her than to see her wed to a poor British captain.

He had been neither happy nor unhappy. He had made his regiment his life and had expected to remain with it until he retired. Then a letter had arrived from a firm of Scottish solicitors.

His uncle, the Earl of Strathairn, a gentleman he had never seen, had died, and, there being no direct heir, Captain Peter

Strange had found himself the new earl and possessed of a handsome fortune. He was promptly released from his regiment so that he might take up his new honours.

He had set sail from India, and, on arriving in England, had immediately travelled to Scotland, first to see the solicitors, and then to survey his domain which lay in the south-west of Scotland, the county of Strathairn, dividing Ayrshire from Renfrewshire. The whole county was only sixty thousand acres but all of it was rich farm land.

His new home, Strathairn Castle, was a Victorian monstrosity of black turrets and towers and pinnacles and arrow slits, all in the mock medieval tradition. It was richly, if gloomily, furnished, and the staff were polite and well-trained. The Chamberlain of Strathairn turned out to be an efficient man called Herbert Jamieson who had required no assistance in running the estates from the late earl and seemed to require no assistance from the new one.

Peter, Lord Strathairn, had, therefore, found himself in that dangerous situation of being a presentable man in the prime of life with a great deal of money at his disposal and very little to occupy his time.

Then a letter had arrived from Mr. Farquharson. Mr. Farquharson, a rich tea planter and his family, had been kind to Captain Peter Strange and had entertained him many times to dinner when he was on leave in Lahore. Mr. Farquharson had written to say he was retired and had returned to his native city, and, having heard of Captain Strange's elevation to the Scottish peerage, had begged him to visit him in Glasgow.

The earl, finding himself bored with inaction and longing for the sights and sounds of India, had promptly accepted the invitation. If he could not return to India, then it would at least be some compensation to talk over old times. Now, he began to wish he had not come. He had, of course, seen dreadful scenes of poverty in India but they had somehow been mitigated by the bright sunshine, and by the fact he *was* in a foreign country, albeit a chunk of the British Empire. It was the evil-smelling darkness of Glasgow on this foggy November day, he decided, which struck such a strange chill into his heart. He felt as if something really quite awful was about to happen.

The carriage lurched and swayed as the horses slipped and stumbled on the greasy, icy cobbles. Lord Strathairn jerked down the window and peered out into the thickening gloom. There seemed to be a tremen-

27

dous amount of traffic, all inching through the suffocating fog. A smell of rank poverty emanated from the looming bulk of the tenements; a smell compounded of cabbage and biscuits, vinegar, coal gas, sour milk and urine.

He drew his head in and slammed up the window as his carriage lurched forward again.

They had only gone a few feet when the carriage stopped again. It had drawn alongside a tall, black brougham which was going in the opposite direction. A young woman looked out, gazing full into the eyes of Lord Strathairn. She was flanked by two grim matrons. It was a haunting face, a wistful face; wide, lost, drowned eyes in a perfect oval of a face; jet-black curls peeping below a modest bonnet. He raised his hat in an involuntary salute, his carriage lurched forward again, and she was gone.

"Ye shouldnae hae done that," said his manservant, Roshie, severely.

"Indeed?" said the earl somewhat haughtily. "And why not?"

"Because thon was Maggie Macleod on her way tae the court," said Roshie with a sort of grim satisfaction. "Her picture's been in a' the papers. The photo wasnae whit ye would ca' a guid likeness, but close enough.

Her husband was an inspector o' police and she poisoned him wi' arsenic."

"Oh," said the earl dismally, sinking his chin into his beaver collar and feeling even more depressed.

Maggie Macleod was weary of life with a soul sickness that ate into every fibre of her being. In a mad way, it did not seem strange to her that she should be on the way to the High Court to stand trial for the murder of her husband. Her marriage seemed to have been one long dreary desert lit by flares of cruelty, rather in the way the harsh gaslight cut through the yellow fog of the streets outside. She had been married only a year before the inspector's death and yet it had seemed like eons.

As the carriage lurched and stopped and lurched and stopped, Maggie remembered her arrival in Glasgow and how stunned she had been by the dirt and noise and endless streets of buildings. The inspector lived in a tall mansion in Park Terrace in the West End of the city. It never dawned on Maggie's innocent mind that her husband lived in a very grand style for a mere police inspector. The house was expensively if tastelessly furnished. Apart from a grim housekeeper, Flora Meikle, there were two housemaids, a parlour maid, an odd job man, and a daily woman to do the heavy work. For one brief moment before her marriage, Maggie had hoped that Inspector Macleod would be kind to her. Her brutal introduction to the mysteries of the marriage bed soon dashed that hope.

The inspector had been married before, that much Maggie had gathered from the housekeeper, Flora Meikle. But as to how or when the late Mrs. Macleod had died, Maggie could never find out. She was too shy to make friends, and, since she was rarely allowed out of the house, had little opportunity to do so.

And then, only two months ago, her life had begun to take a slight turn for the better. Her husband had been closeted in his study, night after night, with the crime reporter of the *Morning Echo*, Murdo Knight, a big, boozy, hard-drinking Scot. The inspector would fall into his bed almost every evening drunk and dead to the world. Maggie was spared his onslaughts of brutal lust. Then Mr. Macleod had begun to give her pin money, suggesting that she take a walk along Sauchiehall Street and look at the shops.

Maggie enjoyed these expeditions although she never dared venture into any of the shops where the assistants looked to her

for already there had been rumours tha
mob, inflamed by the newspaper stor
were ready to tear her to pieces.

The dank smell of the River Clyde bega
to permeate the carriage. They must be near
the court now.

And then Maggie, looking dully out of the
window, saw a face staring at her from a carriage window opposite.

It was a handsome, tanned, rakish face
under the shadow of a tall silk hat. As she
stared at him, his blue eyes twinkled and he
gallantly raised his hat in salute.

And then the carriage moved on.

One of the wardresses muttered 'Masher'
and leaned forward and jerked down the
carriage blind.

Maggie felt her eyes fill with tears. She felt
as if someone had waved to her from some
far-away sunny world on the other side of a
black pit.

Then reality closed in and death, literally,
stared her in the face.

Down under the subterranean passages of
the court, Maggie could hear the din above
her head as people fought for places.

"Time for us to go," said one of the
wardresses, Mrs. Chisholm. She straightened a fold of Maggie's dress and then sur-

country eyes like dukes and duchesses.

She kept the money her husband gave her,
carefully hoarded in a corner of her old tin
trunk. Somewhere in the back of her mind
had been a hope that she could save enough
for a passage to America or Australia. But it
was only a faint little hope. Deep inside she
knew she would never have the courage to
escape.

And then it looked as if her marriage
might become tolerable as her husband became drunker and more jovial. Drink no
longer made him as mean and malicious as
her father. He would plant wet, affectionate
kisses on her mouth and hint he was working on something which would surely make
him superintendent.

But one bitter cold morning he had been
found dead in his study. Flora Meikle, the
housekeeper, had found him and had broken
the news to Maggie, saying it looked as if Mr.
Macleod had died of an apoplexy.

Maggie could still remember that moment when she had stood alone in the bedroom after Flora had left and had realized
that for the first time in her life she was free.

Then the blow had fallen. Mr. Macleod's
doctor, a half blind septuagenarian had
been down with the 'flu and his replace-
ment, Dr. Walker, was young and keen. He

had refused to sign the death certificate, an autopsy had been performed, and the horrified Maggie had learned that her husband had died of arsenic poisoning.

That very day, October first, 1908, Maggie Macleod had been arrested and charged with the murder of her husband. It had been the housemaids' day off and Maggie had made tea for her husband herself. She was examined before Henry Dalzell, Sheriff of Lanarkshire, and then put in prison until she should stand trial.

Flora Meikle loyally supplied Maggie with nourishing meals which she brought to the prison three times a day. Maggie was allowed to wear her own clothes and have the luxury of proper food until such time as she should be found guilty. For it seemed in no doubt that she would be found guilty.

Even the housekeeper seemed to think so, adding to Maggie's torment by supplying her with the daily newspapers which appeared to have condemned her already, particularly Murdo Knight of the *Morning Echo*, who described the sinister look on Maggie's face as she had stared at her husband over the dinner table when he, Murdo, had been a guest. And yet, it was the newspapers that saved Maggie's sanity. Or rather, sanity of a kind. For Maggie had all at once

become convinced that she was going f hanged for a murder she had not mitted, and somehow it seemed only more piece of injustice in an unjust Death began to look attractive. Wit hope, Maggie was able to face her fate.

The fact that there had been no i from her father did not surprise her.

She was to be defended in court by chief counsel, Mr. Andrew Byles, Sheri Inverness, who broke it to her gently that police had evidence that a woman of M gie's description had purchased arseni two apothecary shops in Sauchiehall Stre

Maggie nodded her head as if not s prised at that either. It seemed inevitable her that the net should close so tightly abc her. Mr. Byles took her through her sta ment again, regretting that, under Scotti law, Maggie would not be allowed to spe in her own defence. The girl's sad hones seemed to be the only thing to help prov her innocence.

The brougham taking her from the prisor to the court jerked to a halt again, joltin Maggie back into the immediate present The wardresses were discussing the forthcoming trial. They were blessing the fog and hoping they would be able to get their charge quietly into court by the side door,

veyed her critically like a dresser preparing an actress for her stage appearance.

Maggie had been advised by Flora Meikle to wear her best dress, but Mrs. Chisholm thought Maggie's afternoon dress of fawn silk trimmed with coarse cream lace and silk and cord tassels was a shade too elaborate for a court appearance. But the golden-brown velvet bonnet was neat and modest and framed Maggie's pale face very prettily.

They made their way along dark passages, up a narrow flight of stone stairs and through a trapdoor which led directly into the dock. Maggie blinked in the yellow foggy light of the court and then winced as she felt hundreds of eyes avidly scanning her face.

Had Maggie had any hope of an acquittal left in her tired brain, then surely the sight of the judge would have dashed it.

The trumpeters in their green and gold livery sounded a fanfare and everyone rose as Lord Dancer strolled into court, his white silk robes with their scarlet crosses billowing about his willowy body. His face under his wig was handsome in a cold, high-nosed way, but his strong belief in capital punishment had earned him the name of 'The Grim Reaper'.

Every neck was craned as Maggie — or the panel as the accused is called in Scotland — was placed at the bar. Mr. Ian Macduff, Advocate-Depute conducting the prosecution, put the tips of his fingers together and peered over the steeple made by them at Maggie who was on the other side of the well of the foggy court. The sonorous voice of the clergyman raised in the opening prayer sounded in the sudden tense silence.

Mr. Macduff found himself puzzled. Maggie Macleod was not what he expected.

One enterprising photographer had been on the spot when Maggie had been taken from her home after being charged with murder. His second cousin worked as a nurse in the office of the doctor who had refused to sign the death certificate and so he had learned that something was afoot.

When Maggie had been led from the house the morning had been dark, the pavements and roads gleaming faintly under a coating of frost. The photographer had lit the magnesium powder and had taken a flash picture with his plate camera.

This picture had been sold to all the newspapers. The magnesium flash had made Maggie's face appear a dead-white oval with two black pits for eyes and a shadow distorting her mouth. She had looked decidedly sinister.

But the girl in the dock was beautiful.

Thick black curls rioted under a sober bonnet, and her eyes were large and brown in her white and flawless face. Macduff decided all at once that she looked the very picture of innocent innocence, resigned to a malign fate, and felt the first stirrings of unease.

She exuded an air of soft and virginal femininity, although the girl could hardly be a virgin after being married to a brute like Macleod, reflected Macduff. He glanced up and took a look at Lord Dancer and knew instinctively that the judge had taken a dislike to the girl and, also, that anyone as feminine and appealing as Mrs. Macleod would always bring out the cruel side of the judge's nature.

The jury of fifteen men sat very sober and silent, fifteen pairs of eyes riveted on the accused.

Macduff gave a weary shrug and hitched his gown around his shoulders. He was acting for the Crown and the evidence against Mrs. Macleod was damning. She would hang. The trial was a charade. Nothing more.

Maggie heard the Advocate-Depute's voice begin to read out the indictment. It seemed to come from very far away until all at once her mind grasped what he was saying.

"That albeit, by the laws of this and of

37

every other well-governed realm, the wickedly and feloniously administering of arsenic, or other poison, to any of the lieges, with intent to murder; as also, murder, are crimes of a heinous nature, and severely punishable: yet true it is and of verity, that you, the said Margaret Macleod, or Margaret Fraser Macleod, are guilty of the said crime . . ."

Maggie began to feel faint. Mr. Macduff's voice went inexorably on. ". . . you, the said Margaret Macleod, or Margaret Fraser Macleod, ought to be punished with the pains of law, to deter others from committing the like crimes in all times coming."

"Answer the charges, dear." Mrs. Chisholm, the wardress was whispering in Maggie's ear.

Maggie rose to her feet. It was like being in a nightmare where you wanted to scream but no sound came out.

At last she found her voice.

"Not guilty," said Maggie Macleod.

The trial had begun in earnest.

Three

Mr. Farquharson was just as Lord Strathairn had known him in the Lahore days, plump and rosy and white-haired, lacking only a cotton wool beard and red flannel suit to turn him into the perfect Father Christmas.

His wife also looked the same; small and dark and afflicted with a very yellowish wrinkled complexion under a brittle thatch of red hair. She would not make a very good Mrs. Claus. She looked more like one of the elves.

The earl had hoped for a quiet evening with the Farquharsons, reliving old times among Mr. Farquharson's many mementoes of India; brass ornaments, elephants' feet and stuffed tigers' heads. But Mr. Farquharson had outdone himself in his attempts to provide suitable entertainment for the Earl of Strathairn.

He had invited several members of the Scottish nobility. There was the Honourable Alistair Ashton, young Lord John Robey, and the Marquess of Handley. Female attractions were supplied by the Misses Morag and Sheila Bentley. The guests had all been educated in England, and had accents as English as the earl's own.

The table was groaning under the weight of too many dishes. The Farquharsons did not usually eat dinner in the evening, preferring 'high tea', that meal which consists of one dish and then masses of scones and cakes and buns. They felt the loss of all the usual cakes and pastry and had tried to make up for what they thought was a very stark repast by producing about one meat dish for every missing scone and bun.

Lord Strathairn felt, however, that he might have managed to enjoy the food and the company had not the conversation turned to the trial of that famous poisoner, Maggie Macleod.

It had been a mistake to say he had seen her, for the Misses Bentley gave twittering shrieks of alarm and began to ask whether Mrs. Macleod were as awful as she had appeared in the newspapers and he found himself in the odd position of defending Maggie Macleod. He could not get her face out of his mind.

He was, perhaps, over generous in his praise of her appearance, for the Misses Bentley bridled and waved their fans and looked disappointed in him. They reminded him forcibly of the failures of the London Season with their plain faces and incessant giggles and arch looks.

The men he found pleasant enough, although they too wanted to mull over the Macleod case.

Alistair Ashton was a squat, cheerful young man with a pug face embellished by an old-fashioned Newgate fringe. Lord Robey was thin and pale; pale straw-coloured hair, white eyelashes, pale milky eyes. The Marquess of Handley had a foxy look with his green eyes, long nose and red hair. He had an irritating manner of always seeming to enjoy a private joke.

"It seems pretty definite that the Macleod woman will hang," drawled Lord Robey. "Newspapers are going quite mad about it; silly, little grubby scribe-chappies buzzin' around the High Court like demned wasps. Of course, it is jam for them, murder in high places, don't you know. Police Inspector killed and all that. If it had taken place in the slums, it would have received a paragraph on the bottom of the back page."

"Talking of slums," said Lord Strathairn quickly, anxious to turn the talk away from Maggie Macleod, "there seem to be some very squalid examples in this city. Who owns them? The Glasgow corporation? I am surprised the Press does not turn its gaze on some of the more everyday horrors of this city."

"Most of the slum property is privately owned," said Mr. Farquharson.

"If I were one of the owners," said the earl, "I should not sleep quiet at night."

"Oh, my dear, dear chap," said the Marquess of Handley irritably. "You cannot possibly be as naïve as you appear. There are dreadful slums in London, Birmingham and Manchester, to name only a few places. Where would these creatures live if there were not slums? They are like troglodytes. They adore dark and filth. Poverty is a family disease. They're used to it. If they want to live anywhere better, then they have only to try working for a living for a change."

"But work is very hard to find, I believe," said the earl stubbornly. "I am firmly persuaded they would better themselves if they could. There must be a constant battle against ill health, not to mention . . ."

"Babies," put in Lord Robey with a high laugh. "They breed like rabbits."

"Ladies present," said Mr. Farquharson reprovingly.

"Ah, yes," smiled the Marquess of Handley. "Let us not forget the fair company.

We must be boring them to death."

"If slum conditions bore them to death," said the earl, suddenly disliking the marquess immensely, "then no doubt the murder case at the High Court must also fatigue them." He turned to Mrs. Farquharson and smiled. "My apologies, Mrs. Farquharson. Perhaps I am wrong to be so shocked after a mere glimpse at this city, but I firmly believe that slum owners are worse criminals than Mrs. Macleod and should be made to stand trial for mass murder."

There was an awkward silence, then the marquess laughed. "Well, well, well, a Bolshie has joined the ranks of the peerage."

Lord Strathairn looked at him and surprised a stare of pure hatred in the marquess's green eyes. In a second it was gone, and the marquess was complimenting Miss Morag Bentley on her gown.

The earl sat back in his chair, surprised at his own feelings. He had seen poverty before and had never considered himself to be a reformer of any sort.

Mrs. Farquharson, seeing his frown, rose quickly to her feet as a signal that the gentlemen should be left to their port.

A silence fell on the dinner party after the ladies had left. Mr. Farquharson was quite obviously tired. Then Alistair Ashton began

43

to talk about his experiences with the Lanarkshire and Renfrewshire hunt. Soon the rest were describing their own hunting experiences, the earl describing some of his Indian adventures.

But when the topic was exhausted, there was another restless silence. The earl had a feeling that the three other guests did not normally spend their evenings in such quiet and respectable company. Ashton and Robey were married, that much he had gleaned from earlier conversation, and yet they had not brought their wives, nor it seemed, had their wives been expected. It was almost as if they were using Mr. Farquharson's house as a restaurant, somewhere respectable to dine before they went on to sample the less respectable delights of the night. The Marquess of Handley seemed to be the ringleader for the eyes of the other two would constantly stray towards him as if seeking approval, and they tried to copy Handley's rather effeminate mannerisms and style of dress.

All three wore flowing ties and velvet jackets, affecting a type of genteel Bohemianism.

It was the marquess who suggested that they should join the ladies. The earl frowned in disapproval. Lord Handley should, he felt, have waited for his host to make the suggestion. As he rose from the table, he became aware that his disapproval had been marked by the marquess whose foxy eyes shone with a mocking gleam.

Lord Strathairn began to feel uncomfortable and wondered whether he were becoming a prude.

When they entered the drawing-room, the men noticed with sinking hearts that the candles in their brackets on the pleated silk front of the piano had been lit and that Miss Morag Bentley was to entertain them.

Mrs. Farquharson was asleep, her lace cap tilted over one eye. The men balanced cups of tea on their knees and nibbled at chocolates and blanched almonds, and one and all prayed that Miss Morag did not have an extensive repertoire.

Possibly in honour of the earl she began with a rendering of 'Pale Hands I Loved, Beside the Shalimar'. She had a thin, penetrating voice, slightly off-key. Mrs. Farquharson awoke with a start and immediately leaned forward with a fixed smile of appreciation on her face. Morag's next offering was fortunately not accompanied by her voice. But it was a long, heavy, soporific work involving a lot of business of cross-hands which seemed to go on forever. The earl felt his eyes beginning to droop and jerked them open with an effort.

Slow chord after slow chord crawled across the hot, foggy air. Bands of fog lay across the room through which the massive red plush Victorian furniture looked like great beasts massing for a foray out of the primeval swamp. The gaslights in their brackets hissed and sang, the fire crackled on the hearth, numerous clocks ticked like metronomes, and Mr. Farquharson suddenly let out a stentorian snore.

Miss Morag played on, regardless.

Just when the earl felt he could not bear it any longer, the Misses Bentley's servant arrived to announce their carriage was waiting.

With many arch looks and would-be pretty pouts, the sisters departed in a blast of cold foggy air, since the servant had forgotten to close the street door.

Old Mr. Farquharson was looking very weary indeed and the earl hesitantly suggested they should bring the evening to an end and allow their kind host to go to bed.

The Marquess of Handley put a friendly arm around the earl's shoulders. "I'm sure Farquharson will excuse you if you would care to come with us to The Club for a round of cards. For young fellows like us the night is still young."

The earl hesitated. He was a guest of the Farquharsons and felt he should not go, but Mr. Farquharson was delighted that his young friend appeared to have made a good impression on his other guests and enthusiastically urged him to accept the invitation. The earl glanced at the clock in the corner. Eleven. Well, perhaps only an hour and then he could return.

He reluctantly agreed. Soon he was standing with his new friends on the steps of Mr. Farquharson's home in Sandyford Place, one of the stately terraces on a main road leading up to Charing Cross, and drawing on his gloves.

The fog was still thick. Frost glittered on the pavements and on the black winter trees, lining the road.

He was seized by a strange premonition that he should not go, that somehow this night would change his life, but he put it down to the fog and the strangeness of this black city and fell into step with his companions who had elected to walk to The Club.

For a long time afterwards, the earl was to blame the city of Glasgow itself for the folly of his behaviour of that night.

Normally a cool, level-headed man with all his wits about him, he was, nonetheless, extremely sensitive to atmosphere, and, as he walked along, his footsteps and those of his companions echoing in the silent street, he became aware of a feeling of excitement which seemed to permeate the filthy, frozen air about him; an air of the-devil-take-tomorrow, an air of danger. As the fog thinned, their shadows grew and shortened as they walked under the hissing gas of the street lamps, each surrounded with its own Aurora Borealis of rainbow colours.

Through Charing Cross they went and along Sauchiehall Street, the men stopping to buy the morning papers which were already on the street, on each front page that terrible photograph of Maggie Macleod.

They stopped under a street lamp to read the reports of the day's court proceedings, and the earl felt a sinking feeling of pity for the girl. Her case seemed hopeless. Apothecary James Russell, of 151 Sauchiehall Street had identified her as being the young lady who had bought a quantity of arsenic from him a week before the death of Mr. Macleod, as did apothecary Simon McWhirter of St. George's Cross. Both men said she had signed the book, saying she was going to use the arsenic to put down rats. Mr. Andrew Byles, for the defence, had promptly had the signatures compared with that of Mrs. Macleod and had said triumphantly that they did not match. And with that, Lord Dancer had risen to his feet and had adjourned the case until the morning.

"Now that's a hanging I would like to see," said the marquess.

"Why, in God's name?" exclaimed the earl hotly.

"You must not take me seriously," mocked the marquess. He turned to his friends. "Can it be that our new friend, Strathairn, has a soft spot for the girl?"

They all laughed and linked arms with the earl, forcing him to walk along with them at a smart pace. There seemed to be drunks everywhere, lurching in and out of the shadows.

A barefoot woman with a baby wrapped in a shawl stopped them and said something to the marquess in an accent so broad that the earl could not make out a word she was saying.

"Hey, Constable!" shouted the marquess in a loud voice. "Police, I say!"

The woman gave him a terrified look and ran away into the concealing fog, clutching the baby tightly, while the marquess roared with laughter and Alistair Ashton and Lord Robey looked uncomfortable.

"Just imagine," said the marquess cheerfully as they resumed their fast walk, "soliciting while carrying a baby, no less, and as ugly and dirty as sin. She *deserves* to be arrested."

The earl stopped and said in a level voice, "That poor woman probably needed money for food. There was no need to frighten her so. This whole place stinks of poverty."

There was a startled little silence and then Lord Robey laughed awkwardly. "Don't distress yourself," he said. "As I said earlier, poverty is a disease. These people could better themselves if they wanted to. Hey, we are nearly there. It's called The Club because there is no other club in Glasgow worth belonging to."

They turned off Sauchiehall Street and walked down Hope Street for some yards and stopped outside a large grey building where lights still burned behind closed blinds.

By this time the earl would not have been surprised to find himself in a gambling hell, but The Club appeared to be the epitome of respectability with smooth green carpets and large leather chairs stretched out under the blazing white light of the gaseliers. They left their hats and coats with the porter, the earl was signed in as an honorary member, and the marquess led the way to the card room.

It was an odd room, being quite small and papered with a heavy flock wallpaper. The windows were of green, brown and gold stained glass portraying various ladies with long brown hair holding water lilies in their long, white pointed fingers like so many Ladies of Shalott about to step into the barge to bear them down to many tower'd Camelot.

Baccarat was the choice of game, which rather surprised the earl since he knew it was forbidden by law. Of course, everyone played it at country house parties and places like that, but he had not expected it to be so openly allowed in such a seemingly respectable provincial club.

The earl had drunk a great deal already that evening since Mr. Farquharson was an extremely generous host and appeared to have a bottomless capacity for claret. Although the earl diluted his whisky with soda, it seemed to go straight to his head, and the strange room took on an even more unreal air as the fog crept through the cracks of the windows and the gas fire hissed and popped and the gaselier above his head sent down a tremendous heat.

He found himself beginning to lose very heavily, a new experience for him since he had always been clever and lucky at cards and had been able to supplement his small income in India with his skill.

After some time, Lord Robey and Alistair Ashton retired from the game. The earl realized that he, Peter, fourth Earl of Strathairn, was becoming very drunk indeed, and, with his pleasant voice slightly slurred, he asked to be allowed to retire also.

"Havers, as they say in this part of the world," said the marquess, his narrow green eyes glinting. "I tell you what, this playing for money is a bore. We've all got so much of it. Now, I have a suggestion to make. You and I, Strathairn, will play for something more exciting. Are you game?"

"Provided it's just one more hand," said the earl wearily.

"Fine. Right. Well, it's like this," said the Marquess of Handley with his irritating, mocking smile, "we play for the hand in marriage of Maggie Macleod. Loser has to marry her."

There was a stunned silence. The four men were the only occupants of the card room. Alistair Ashton let out a high, nervous bark of laughter.

Lord Robey stifled a yawn. "Handley's joking," he said. "Let's all go home."

"No, I'm not joking." Handley shuffled the cards expertly. "Let me fill up your glass,

Strathairn. Hey, what the devil . . . !" He stared at the door. The other three men swung around. There was no one there.

"Oh, it was nothing," said the marquess, pushing a glass of whisky towards the earl. "I thought I saw someone who is supposed to be in Australia. Come along, Strathairn. You must have played for wilder stakes when you were in India."

"Oh," said the earl with a reminiscent smile, "we played for all sorts of mad things. I remember once the loser had to swim the . . ." He gave his head a shake. He had suddenly become almost abnormally sleepy. All at once, his memory went. Why was Handley staring at him so expectantly? What was he saying now?

The marquess's voice seemed to come from a long way away. "Well," he was saying impatiently, "shall we play?"

Lord Strathairn looked at him wearily. It was something about one more game. "Very well," he said sleepily. "So long as it's only one hand."

The marquess rang the bell and asked the servant to bring the betting book. The earl rallied enough to say, "What do we need the betting book for?"

"As you will see," said the marquess, languidly dismissing the servant who had en-

53

tered. "We'll just sign a bit of paper and Robey and Ashton here will witness it. All good fun, of course."

"Of course," echoed the earl. "Oh, let's get it over with. I'm dog-tired."

The room swam out of focus. The earl clutched at the edge of the table and shook his head to clear it. He realized he must have drunk far too much but he was damned if he would disgrace himself by showing he could not carry his drink in front of such a cad as Handley. He saw the blur of a piece of paper in front of him and shakily affixed his signature.

He automatically drank the glass at his elbow and tried to concentrate on the game. But voices seemed to ebb and flow and, he was not quite sure how it happened, but all at once he was being helped to his feet, and the marquess was laughing and slapping him on the back and saying he would see him at the wedding.

He felt himself falling and clutched at a chair back for support. But a great black void rushed up to swallow him and he plunged into unconsciousness.

He awoke some time the next morning with only a hazy recollection of the evening's events. His head ached like the very devil and his mouth was a dry and raging furnace.

At first he could not think where he was until his manservant, Roshie, came quietly into the room and opened the curtains and placed a cup of tea and two Osborne biscuits on the bedside table. Roshie had been the late earl's gentleman's gentleman and Lord Strathairn had inherited him along with the estate.

"Where am I, Roshie?" asked the earl faintly.

"Ye're in Mr. Farquharson's in Glasgow and ye wis carried hame in the wee hours," said Roshie gloomily.

"Oh, God." The earl sat up in bed and clutched his head.

"Furthermair, that there Marquess o' Handley is doonstairs waitin' fur your lordship. Now, I ken I shouldnae speak ill o' ma betters, but that cheil . . ."

"It's all right, Roshie. I know what you mean. Give me my dressing gown and send his lordship up here. I'll soon be shot of him."

He propped himself against the pillow and thirstily drank his tea, wishing he had asked Roshie to bring the whole pot.

The door opened and the earl stared coldly at his visitor. "Well, Handley, what brings you calling so early?"

"Why, to see you wed, old boy," grinned the marquess, tossing his top hat onto the bed.

"I haven't the faintest idea what you're talking about."

"Don't you remember our last game of cards? Loser marries Maggie Macleod?"

"Nonsense. I would never make such a bet. Go away. My head aches."

Still grinning, the marquess pulled a piece of paper from his pocket and handed it to the earl.

The earl read it several times as if he could not believe the evidence of his eyes. But there it was. He, Peter, Lord Strathairn, had solemnly promised to wed Maggie Macleod.

He turned white. "You cannot keep me to such a bet."

"But I can, my dear fellow. You signed the paper, and I've a great wish to see you married. You'll be a widower soon enough. She's bound to hang."

"And if I refuse?"

The marquess's green eyes narrowed. "If you refuse, laddie, I'll have your wager published in all the newspapers. It is the first time I have had to argue with a *gentleman* about honouring his bets."

Lord Strathairn swung his legs out of bed and shrugged himself into his dressing-gown. The slip of paper with his bet on it fell to the floor and the marquess stooped and picked it up.

"I should have torn that up," said the earl.

"And what a better story that would have made," retorted the marquess. "We have two witnesses, you know."

"Oh, publish and be damned," said the earl wrathfully, unconsciously quoting the Duke of Wellington.

"Really? Have you no care for your reputation? In your new position you would never live down the scandal. On the other hand, if you marry the girl, I'll make sure nobody knows about it."

The earl ran his fingers through his thick fair hair. He had not realized until just this moment how seriously he did take his title and the social responsibilities that went with it. He had been warned by the solicitors that although his estates in Scotland lay in the south-west, rather than in the Highlands, he still might encounter a certain amount of suspicion and resentment because of his English birth. But, they had added, a display of responsibility and concern towards his new tenants would soon dispel that.

What on earth would the whole county of Strathairn think if they read in the newspapers that shortly after his inheritance he had gone into Glasgow to get drunk, gamble, and indulge in tasteless bets? If he could not hold his drink like a gentleman, then at least he could behave like one. Still, the whole affair was like some bad dream.

"But why?" he burst out suddenly. "*Why* are you doing this to me?"

The marquess surveyed him blandly. "Because it amuses me," he said. "You're a little too priggish for my taste, my friend."

"But how can such a thing be kept quiet? There will need to be a minister or priest. A special licence. That sort of thing."

"This is Scotland," said the marquess. "It's enough to stand before two witnesses and announce you're married and the deed is done. It's a game, laddie, a game. Dinnae fash yersel, as the peasants say in this neck of the woods."

"Are you quite serious about putting it in the newspapers?"

"Oh yes," said the marquess softly. "Oh, yes."

The earl thought furiously. He tried to remember the events of the night before but could not.

At last he looked full at the marquess, his blue eyes blazing. "Damn you," he said. "I'll go through with it, but before I do, then you, Handley, and your friends will sign a paper promising to keep quiet about it."

"Gladly," said the marquess smoothly. "I have it here, you see. I felt sure our written word would make you feel better about the delicacy and secrecy of the whole business."

He produced the paper like a conjurer. He had forged Alistair Ashton and Lord Robey's signatures himself, since he could not be bothered going in search of the two young men on a freezing cold foggy morning. He prided himself, however, on his foresight. He had been sure the earl would demand such a promise, if only to salve his pride. The marquess considered himself a good judge of men. He had been frightened that Lord Strathairn would prove to be too difficult for him to handle, but he turned out to be as easy as all the rest. It was a joy to torment him like this. Not only was Strathairn a sickening prig, he was an Englishman, and the Marquess of Handley hated the English with almost as much venom as his Jacobite ancestors.

The earl put down the paper containing the pledge of secrecy and asked, "How is such a marriage to be achieved?"

"I have made arrangements for you to visit Mrs. Macleod in her cell at the High Court during the dinner recess," said the marquess. "Dinner is eaten in the middle of the day in this town. I have spoken to her advocate, Mr. Byles. He will be there, and so will I."

"She will probably refuse. What then?" asked the earl.

"In that case, you will have fulfilled your part of the bet and all can be forgotten."

The earl studied the marquess's foxy face and began to wonder whether the man were mad. But then society in London went to endless lengths to play malicious practical jokes on each other. This could not be happening to him. He must not allow it to happen. He could ring for the servants and have Handley thrown out and then take himself off to the South of France until the scandal died down. But he had been brought up on the rigid principles of what a gentleman could do and what he could not do. A gentleman always honoured his bets. No use blaming Handley for the whole thing. But why, oh why, had he, Peter Strathairn, become so abominably, stupidly drunk?

Aloud, he asked, "What is an advocate?"

"A barrister."

"Then why not say so?"

"Scottish law is based on Roman law. It's different from English law which is based on Common law. There are fifteen on the jury, for example, not twelve, and there is no opening speech by the prosecution out-lining the case and the Crown's assumption of guilt. No indication is made of what form the prosecution will take. There are different names and different procedures."

The earl walked to the window and stared out at the blackness of the day outside and at the gaslights burning in the streets below. "What o'clock is it?" he asked over his shoulder. "It looks like the middle of the night."

"Eleven o'clock in the morning, my lord," said Roshie, coming quietly into the room and beginning to lay out his master's clothes.

"What a filthy climate," said the earl bitterly.

Roshie primmed up his mouth in disapproval. "Weel, the winters in Scotland are aye a bit dark on account o' the lang nights, and o' course in the city, ye get a big o' fog that disnae help, but the summers, it hardly ever gets dark. If his lordship would care to wait below until ye're barbered, my lord . . ."

"Yes," said the earl hurriedly. "I'll join you presently, Handley, and get this matter over with as soon as possible."

Roshie's eyes narrowed in his brown, wrinkled face as he looked past his master to the marquess who was polishing his top hat on his cuff.

"Are ye no' havin' a bite o' breakfast, my lord?"

"No," said the earl with a shudder. "I couldn't eat a thing."

"Aye, weel, now. Wherevers ye're going, you'll be takin' me."

"No, Roshie. I shall not need you."

Roshie began to strop the razor, looking as if he would like to slit the Marquess of Handley's throat with it. As he often said afterwards, he knew that something bad was afoot.

Their footsteps echoed hollowly on the stone flags of the passage leading to the cells under the High Court.

The earl felt ill. Everything seemed divorced from reality. The marquess walked in front of him, and Mr. Byles, the Sheriff of Inverness, behind. He felt as if he had just been arrested.

The day outside was black and foggy. Mr. Byles reflected sourly on the morning's proceedings in court. He felt he would like to strangle Flora Meikle, the Macleods' housekeeper.

Flora obviously believed in telling the whole truth and nothing but the truth, so that when asked if there had been anything in her mistress's manner which would lead the housekeeper to believe that she could be capable of murder, the grim Flora sniffed and said she considered most people capable of murder, somehow, thereby giving the impression that she believed her mistress guilty but was loyally begging the question. Asked if Mrs. Macleod had made tea for her husband herself, Flora had replied, "Yes, certainly, but she did not put anything in it." But when asked if she had seen Mrs. Macleod make the tea and carry it in to her husband, Flora had again sniffed and remarked sourly that she had more to do with her time. Every inch of her rigid being emanated loyalty to Maggie Macleod, but it was a loyalty which contained no personal warmth. It was the loyalty of a good servant who prided herself on always behaving as a good servant should. She had made a most unsympathetic witness.

And now, thought Mr. Byles bitterly, there was this earl wishing to marry Mrs. Macleod. He was probably insane, but the Marquess of Handley had great power, so it would not do to cross him and he was obviously urging Strathairn in his folly. Mr. Byles stole a look at the earl's face. It was a strong handsome face with a good chin and firm mouth. He did not look at all like the type of man who would want to be in the same room with Handley, let alone allow him to join in this idiotic scheme. But a lot of very honest and respectable people entertained Handley. Had he been plain Mr. Jones, reflected Byles, then everyone would at once see him for what he was — a poisonous, plotting, evil man. But they only saw the title and a peerage seemed to cover its owner in a sort of rosy glow. Ah, well, Maggie Macleod had the hangman to face so she would probably consider a proposal of marriage trivial by comparison.

A warder, standing at attention outside one of the cells, saluted smartly and unlocked the door. The earl felt his mouth go dry.

Maggie Macleod rose to her feet as they entered. Mr. Byles jerked his head at the wardress who had been sitting with her, and the woman quietly left the room.

"Visitors for you, Mrs. Macleod," said Mr. Byles.

Maggie's eyes flew to the earl's face. There was a sudden flash of recognition. Her face was very white against the black frame of her hair and the black bombazine of her severe gown. She had gone against Flora Meikle's advice, deciding that mourning was more suitable. Her hair was severely dressed, falling in two smooth wings from a central parting and fastening in a knot at the nape of her neck.

"And what can I do for you, gentlemen?" Her voice was soft and lilting.

Mr. Byles cleared his throat awkwardly. "Mrs. Macleod, may I present the Marquess of Handley and the Earl of Strathairn. My lords . . . Mrs. Macleod." Both men bowed and Maggie executed a low curtsy.

Somewhere up above in the street outside a drunk was howling 'Bonnie Mary of Argyll'. A sharp voice was then heard telling him to shut up, and a silence fell in the narrow cell.

The air was clammy and cold and smelled of fog and Jeyes Fluid.

The Marquess of Handley nudged Mr. Byles with his elbow. Mr. Byles started, cleared his throat, and said, "Mrs. Macleod, his lordship, the Earl of Strathairn, is desirous of marrying you."

Her large brown eyes widened, looked startled, and then filled with bitter contempt. "Another one," she said wearily.

All through the court proceedings, she had carried in her mind that little golden picture of the man in the carriage who had gallantly saluted her. And now he was here before her. And he was as twisted and deformed in soul as all the rest. Before her marriage, her life had not been happy, but it had been bearable. She should never have drugged her father's whisky that night. God was punishing her, as she had known He would.

"Another?" echoed the earl.

"Oh, yes," sighed Maggie. "They come by every post. Proposals, that is."

There was an awkward silence.

"Yes, yes," said the marquess testily, after a pause. "But this is a lord and a gentleman who wants to marry you."

"Ah, and I should be flattered? What is the point of this bad joke, my lords? If I marry my lord here, he will shortly find himself a widower."

The earl walked forward and took her hand in his. "Look here," he began. "I don't like this any more than you do . . ."

"Then why are you doing it?" her soft voice interrupted him. She gently removed her hand and hid it in the folds of her skirt.

The earl shrugged impatiently. The narrow confines of the cell made him feel claustrophobic. He felt trapped in some medieval nightmare. He said harshly, "Just answer one question, Mrs. Macleod. Will you marry me or not?"

She raised her eyes and studied his face for a long time. Maggie was almost willing him to change back into the man of her dreams instead of this dilettante who amused himself in a criminal cell. But he did not look amused. He looked . . . he looked as if he were hoping like mad that she would refuse.

Maggie's glance travelled to the Marquess of Handley's face. He was watching the earl with a sort of avid, gleeful look. She suddenly thought she had the answer. It was merely some sort of casual joke. Let's pass this dreary, foggy morning by going and proposing to Maggie Macleod.

To her own ears, her voice seemed to come from very far away, as if it belonged to another person, a person who said calmly, "Yes, I will marry you. I have a mind to go to my grave a countess."

She caught a look of disappointment on the earl's face and answered it with a little nod of her head as if what she had seen there had answered her unspoken question.

"Very well," said the marquess gleefully. "First, it must be understood that no one is to know of this marriage. It is to be kept secret."

"Of course," said Maggie. "You would not want the world to know what great fools you are making of yourselves."

"That's enough of that," said the marquess

sharply. "Do you agree to keep silent?"

She spread out her small hands in a submissive gesture. "Why not?" she said. "The hangman will silence me soon enough."

"Then," said the marquess, looking at her with dislike, "it is enough that you state in front of me and Mr. Byles that you are man and wife."

Maggie's face had gone totally blank. She performed her part of the ridiculously brief ceremony with complete indifference. Once again, the reality of death faced her, and if it amused these men to humiliate her, then it was of no matter.

The warder rattled his keys impatiently outside the cell and Mr. Byles said, "We must go, my lords."

Above their heads, a bell rang shrilly for the start of the afternoon's court proceedings.

The earl turned in the doorway of the cell, and said, "Mrs. Macleod . . ."

"You forget," she corrected gently, "I am now the Countess of Strathairn."

"Yes, but that's a secret among the four of us," said Mr. Byles hurriedly. "Come along, my lords."

The earl suddenly wanted to convey to Maggie how this mad proposal had come about, but she had picked up a small Bible and had started to read. As the cell door slammed behind them, he felt sure she had already dismissed them all from her mind. Maggie Macleod was preparing her soul for death.

Mr. Byles went one way to enter the court, and the marquess and the earl left by a side door which led out of the building.

Fog swirled about the two men as they stepped out into the street; choking, dense fog.

"Well, Strathairn," mocked the marquess. "How does it feel to be married?"

The earl swung his fist and smashed the marquess full on the end of his long nose with such force that he catapulted across the greasy cobbles and fell on his bottom in the mud.

"You'll regret this," hissed the marquess, mopping the blood streaming down his face with a large handkerchief.

"Hear this, Handley," said the earl, walking forwards, catching him by his flowing ascot, and jerking him roughly to his feet. "One day, you'll curse the day you ever met me." Then he threw the marquess away from him and stalked off down the street.

The earl felt cold and depressed and sick. Had he not felt so ill, he felt sure he would have been able to find a way out of honouring such an atrocious bet. Little bits of the night before came back to him in brief flashes, like the lights of the shops seen through the shifting fog. Then the thought struck him that the marquess would be every bit as reluctant to receive publicity about the bet as he was himself and he cursed himself for a gullible fool.

He hesitated at a corner of the street, wondering which way to go. He was reluctant to return to the Farquharsons and face Roshie's questioning gaze.

He remembered guiltily that he had left his host's house without saying where he was going and when he would return. Although it was only a little past lunchtime, the evening editions of the papers were on sale, and he bought two from a newsvendor, then pushed open the door of a pub in Ingram Street and escaped out of the cold fog.

Most of the people were finishing their dinner — dinner being taken at lunchtime and high tea in the evening. The room was rather like a railway train, being split up into a line of booths. He selected an empty one, realizing he was very hungry. He looked at the menu wondering what on earth cock-a-leekie soup might be — and what on earth were neeps? He finally decided on a plate of roast mutton and a tankard of beer, giving his order to the waiter, and spreading out the newspapers he had bought on the table.

Both had managed to get artists into court and both carried sketches of Maggie Macleod. They were surprisingly good, the artists each in their way having managed to capture her look of lost, childlike innocence. The earl realized with a jolt that not for one minute had he ever considered her guilty, despite the damning evidence against her. The trial, he read, was expected to finish on the following morning.

When his food arrived, he ate steadily and conscientiously, trying to blot out from his mind that he was a married man, shortly to become a widower. Although the articles about Maggie were more sympathetic than previous articles had been, they still seemed to expect her to be found guilty.

One of the newspapers, more enterprising than the others, had gone to Maggie's home and had unearthed the strange story of her marriage. Several of the townspeople of Beauly were quoted as saying that John Fraser had shut up shop and fled when he had heard the news of his daughter's arrest. They also said that Maggie had been brutally treated as a child, and, in their opinion, she had been *sold* to the inspector by the grocer.

At last he finished his meal and plunged out into the city of eternal night. A hansom loomed up in the fog and he asked the driver to take him back to Sandyford Place. He apologized to Mr. Farquharson for his absence, saying he had dined.

Mr. Farquharson looked troubled, and, at last, asked his guest to join him for a drink in his study.

The elderly Scotsman lit the gas fire and poured two glasses of whisky into heavy crystal goblets and then sat down opposite the earl with a worried look on his normally cheerful face.

"I hope nothing untoward happened last night," Mr. Farquharson began.

"Why should it?" The earl swirled the amber liquid round his glass and avoided his old friend's gaze.

"Well, I didn't want to ask Handley to dinner and that's a fact. Now Robey and Ashton are nice young men. They're both lately married and not yet used to being tied down. But they'll settle all right. But Handley . . . there's always been something unsavoury about Handley. Nothing that I could say for sure. But he more or less invited himself. I hope he didn't get up to any mischief."

The earl had a sudden longing to tell him

everything, but he was bitterly ashamed of his stupidity, and pride kept him silent.

"No, nothing," he said lightly. "We played cards at The Club, that is all."

"Oh, well . . ." Mr. Farquharson looked more cheerful. "Did you take a fancy to either of the Bentley girls? They're fine lassies with a good dowry apiece."

"I have not had enough time to form an opinion," said the earl cautiously.

"That's just what I was saying to Martha," said Mr. Farquharson. Martha was his wife. "I said, our young lord didn't really have a chance to get to talk to either of them. I'll tell you what I'll do. We'll have an impromptu little soirée tonight, and the ladies can perform for you. They live quite near so it's only a matter of sending . . ."

"No!" said Peter. "I mean, that would be splendid normally and I should look forward to it no end, but the fact is I am feeling terrible. I drank too much last night and all I want is a quiet evening with yourself and Mrs. Farquharson."

"Well, well. If that's your wish. I have a wee bit of excitement to offer you tomorrow, bye the bye. I have managed to get us seats in court to hear the end of the Macleod trial."

The earl closed his eyes. Already in his mind he had been planning to go to

London, to put as far a distance between himself and Glasgow as possible. But, he reflected wryly, at least he should attend and see the last of his wife before the judge put on the black cap.

There was nothing he could do to save her. He had no influence in high places. She had the best counsel she could possibly have — even the newspapers admitted that.

An appeal! Surely he could petition for a stay of execution at the very least? That was something he could do. And that meant staying on in Glasgow.

"Why?" demanded the earl suddenly. "Why on earth come here to retire? Scotland is full of so many beautiful places."

Mrs. Farquharson looked amused. "Don't be too hard on Glasgow. So far you've seen it at its worst, what with the fog and the freezing weather. But there's something about it that always brings you back. The people, I think. I often think they are the noisiest, drunkenest, funniest, *kindest* people in the whole world."

"They are not very kind to Maggie Macleod."

"Och, if the girl's innocent, they'll not be letting her hang. You'll see."

He's talking about my wife, thought the earl. *Maggie Macleod is my wife!*

Four

The newspapers, who were unfortunately allowed to try, sentence and condemn anyone they pleased, had subtly changed their attitude towards Maggie Macleod. A note of reluctant admiration for the brave young figure in the dock had crept into their reports. More emphasis was put on the vast disparity between her age and that of her late husband. The inspector had been fifty-four. It was pointed out in the Press that her signature did not match the signatures in the apothecaries' books, and, if Mrs. Macleod had been guilty, then surely she would have signed a false name.

But it was evident from the opening of the last day of the trial that High Court judge, Lord Dancer, did not share the views of the reporters who were already crowding the Press bench. As the trumpeters sounded their opening fanfare he strolled into the court, nonchalantly swinging the black cap in his hand.

In England, the black cap that the judge

donned when pronouncing sentence of death was a small affair, a piece of black silk. But in Scotland the judge donned a black tricorne, like an old-fashioned highwayman's hat, and many who had seen 'The Grim Reaper' donning it before said he wore it with an air and at just the correct angle, as if he had practised putting it on in his bedroom looking-glass.

The earl sat with Mr. Farquharson near the front of the court. Maggie Macleod sat pale and silent in the dock. If she had noticed him, she gave no sign of it.

Fog, that ever-present choking fog, laid its pale fingers across the gloom of the courtroom as Mr. Ian Macduff, Advocate-Depute, rose to present the case for the Crown. It was a damning summing up and the earl felt all his hopes of Maggie being acquitted ebb away.

Maggie Macleod had made the tea for her husband and carried it in to him. On her own admission, she had been alone in the kitchen. Two apothecaries had identified her as the young woman who had purchased a quantity of arsenic at their shops a week before the death of Mr. Macleod.

The servants had testified that Mrs. Macleod at no time showed any emotion towards her husband other than fear, and yet there was no evidence that Mr. Macleod had mistreated his wife in any way.

Maggie thought briefly of the humiliations of the marriage chamber and closed her eyes.

Crime reporter, Murdo Knight, had testified that Mrs. Macleod had often looked at her husband "as if she would like to kill him" and Mr. Macduff would remind the gentlemen of the jury of Mr. Knight's reputation as being a fair and accurate reporter.

As it went on, Maggie withdrew her mind from the proceedings. She felt nothing now but a great empty numbness. The brief glimpse she had had of the earl had done nothing to her senses at all. He already belonged to the past.

Outside, the fog began to swirl and stream alongside the black tenements as a rising wind blew all the way from the Gulf Stream. Although it was November, it was one of those warm damp winds which frequently descend on the streets of Glasgow, bringing with it a false taste of spring.

The wind rose higher outside the court. On the River Clyde, the tall masts of the shipping began to toss and sway as if some bare pine forest had come to life. Higher it rose, tearing the fog to shreds, melting the frost from the roads and pavements, booming in the closes and wynds, scrubbing the city clean.

As Mr. Byles rose to speak for the defence, a watery sun shone through the grimy window panes, casting one broad band of golden light onto the pale oval of Maggie Macleod's face.

It seemed as if hope and life and youth had come blowing all the way in from the Clyde estuary, all the way from the Atlantic.

Maggie felt the warm sun on her cheek and suddenly she seemed to be struggling in a nightmare. Destructive hope flew into her heart and she could hardly restrain herself from crying out, "I'm innocent! What are you doing to me? I'm innocent!"

Her wide, trapped eyes flew here and there about the court, seeking help, seeking freedom.

Mr. Byles was brilliant in his defence . . . or rather it would have been a brilliant defence had he not been constantly interrupted by Lord Dancer.

"The lady who bought the arsenic from the two apothecaries' shops has been described as wearing a lavender wool gown with a black mantle trimmed with sable. Mrs. Macleod does not possess garments such as these, and this has been confirmed by her servants . . ."

"She would no doubt have got rid of the

clothes which would help to identify her," interrupted Lord Dancer in a conversational tone.

Mr. Byles faltered in his address to the jury, swore under his breath, and continued. He laid great stress on the fact that Mrs. Macleod's signature did not match the signatures in the apothecaries' books.

"Disguised handwriting?" murmured his lordship, cleaning his nails with a steel pen.

"Nor, had she been guilty, would she have signed her own name," pursued Mr. Byles.

"No one has said she was a *practised* criminal," interrupted Lord Dancer impatiently.

And so it went on. Nonetheless, Mr. Byles did his best, and very good it was too. But the judge's interruptions *did* flummox him and several times he had to pause and consult his notes, feeling that the sympathy of the jury had been lost.

When he finally sat down, Lord Dancer delicately cleared his throat and commenced his summing up. It was more like a speech for the prosecution thought the earl, gritting his teeth.

The jury of fifteen sat stolidly, staring up at the judge. It was impossible to know what they were thinking.

Lord Dancer's cultured and charming voice went on and on.

"She'll hang, as sure as eggs are eggs," muttered Mr. Farquharson. The earl turned quite pale. Watching him out of the corner of his eye, Mr. Farquharson began to wish he had not brought his young friend to this trial. But who would have thought that Captain Peter Strange would be so squeamish?

Lord Dancer fingered the silk of his robes and turned his pale gaze on the jury.

"It may create the greatest reluctance in your mind to take any other view of the matter than that she was guilty of administering arsenic poisoning. Now the great and invaluable use of a jury, after they direct their minds seriously to the case with the attention you have done, is to separate suspicion from evidence. And, therefore, if you cannot say we find here satisfactory evidence that the poison *must* have been administered by her — whatever may be your suspicion, however heavy the weight and load of suspicion is against her, and however you may have to struggle to get rid of it, you perform the best and bounden duty as a jury to separate suspicion from truth, and to proceed upon nothing that you do not find established in evidence against her.

"But," he went on, leaning forward, his shoulders hunched up in his robes creating the illusion of a bird of prey, "if, on the other hand you return a verdict satisfactory to yourselves against the prisoner, you need not fear any consequences from any future, or imagined, or fancied discovery which may take place. You have done your duty under your oaths, under God, and to your country, and may feel satisfied that remorse you can never have."

Then he placed the black cap conspicuously on the bench in front of him, as if wishing to remove any last lingering doubt from the minds of the jury as to what their verdict should be.

The jury of fifteen men retired, heads bowed. Not one of them looked at Maggie. "A bad sign," Mr. Farquharson was about to say until the sight of the earl's tense face stopped him.

Maggie Macleod, it was noted, refused to retire, preferring to stay in the dock and wait for the sentence.

Mr. Farquharson drew out his enormous cigar case. "Let's step outside and get a breath of air and a smoke," he whispered. The earl shook his head. "You go," he said, and Mr. Farquharson, after a worried look at his friend, arose and shuffled his way along to the end of the bench.

Peter, Lord Strathairn, sat with his arms folded across his chest, waiting for the bell to sound which would signal the return of the jury. He was glad the Marquess of Handley was not present. Things were bad enough without that horrible individual, sitting waiting like a vulture.

At that moment, the Marquess of Handley, Lord Robey and Alistair Ashton were playing billiards in a saloon in West Princes Street. The marquess had been in fine form, chatting of this and that before the game. But when it was over and they were putting their cues up on the rack, Alistair Ashton said suddenly, "Robey and I got to talking about the other night, Handley."

"Indeed," said the marquess with his foxy smile. "You mean the night of Strathairn's downfall?"

"Exactly," chimed in Lord Robey. "You didn't make him go through with it, did you Handley?"

"A bet's a bet," said the marquess, shrugging his shoulders into his coat.

"But not *such* a bet," said Alistair Ashton. "The man was drunk and didn't know what he was doing."

The marquess laughed. "What a marvellous day. I'll always remember it. Johnnie Robey and Alistair Ashton preaching morality."

Lord Robey's thin, weak face looked suddenly grim. He put his hand in his pocket and drew out an ace of spades and held the card up. "I took this as a souvenir of the game, Handley," he said, staring at the marquess and running his thumb gently over the card. "See! Little pinpricks. Marked cards. And the porter at The Club handed this to me last night. Said you'd dropped it. It's a bottle of chloral. So what Alistair and I want to know is why you marked the cards and why you drugged Strathairn?"

The marquess looked quickly around. "Nonsense!" he said. "It was just a bit of a joke." His mind worked rapidly. Maggie Macleod would hang. No one would ever hear of his part in the marriage.

"I don't see what you're both looking so solemn for," he laughed. "You don't think for a minute that I made Strathairn go through with it."

Alistair Ashton looked at the marquess thoughtfully. "I hope you didn't," he said. "But I'll tell you one thing, Handley. Johnnie and me, well, we've decided we won't be seeing you for a bit."

"Suit yourselves," said the marquess.

"And, furthermore," put in Lord Robey, "I think it would be a good idea if you resigned your membership of The Club."

The wind howled and rattled along the street outside and a shop sign creaked mournfully as it swung to and fro.

The marquess ducked his head before a greenish mirror in the corner and adjusted his silk hat.

"Look here you two," he said over his shoulder. "Before you start lecturing me on morals and demanding my resignation from The Club, just think on this. You have been my guests many times at a certain charming little house in Renfield Street. I am sure Madame Dupont remembers you both vividly. Now, you would not like your delightful wives to know what you get up to in that establishment?"

"Bastard," said Lord Robey. "You have no proof."

"On the contrary, I have plenty of proof. You have no idea how these girls will talk for a few shillings. It would amuse them to call on your wives and families."

The marquess studied their faces and smiled. He swung round and held out his hand. "My property, I think, my *very* dear boy," grinned the marquess, taking the ace of spades and the bottle of chloral from Lord Robey's nerveless fingers.

"Run along, little boys," mocked the marquess. "And before you think of cutting me

in public, do remember that I enjoy revenge. Witness the downfall of the priggish
Strathairn. Ah, sweet revenge, quite my favourite pastime, I assure you . . ."

Mr. Farquharson edged his plump figure
into the space next to the earl and whispered, "Are you sure you wouldn't like to
leave for a bit? They say the jury's going to
be a long while."

The earl shook his head, his eyes straying
to where Maggie sat in the dock. There was
a faint sheen of tears in her eyes. The blus-
tery wind which howled about the building
was making the courtroom full of people
restless.

"Poor thing," said a woman behind the
earl. "She looks as if she's jist realized she's
for the lang drop. I sweer, she didnae do it.
My mither's neighbour, Aggie Benson, said
she kenned auld Macleod and it waud be jist
like the auld scunner tae take the poison
hisself just to spite folks."

The wait seemed endless. "Maybe they'll
not be deciding anything until tomorrow,"
said Mr. Farquharson in a louder voice.
Like everyone else in the court, he was getting tired of whispering.

Perhaps it was Maggie Macleod herself
who was causing the restless atmosphere as

well as the change in the weather. When she had appeared numb and lifeless, it had been easy for the crowd to enjoy the drama of the court without considering that a young girl's life was at stake. But now that she had come alive, the wait seemed doubly endless.

The earl no longer stopped to consider that an acquitted Maggie meant he would be a married man. His lips moved in soundless prayer, "Dear God, if there is a God, let her go free."

The bell to announce the return of the jury rang suddenly and violently.

"This is it," said Mr. Farquharson.

Maggie Macleod straightened her back and looked straight in front of her.

The jury had only been out for an hour. As they shuffled into their seats again, the earl studied their faces. All of them were looking ox-like, except the foreman who stood nervously, holding a piece of paper.

"Have you decided on your verdict, gentlemen?" asked Lord Dancer, one white, well-manicured hand reaching towards the black cap.

"We have, my lord."

"And do you find the panel guilty or not guilty of the charge of murder?"

"Not proven, my lord."

"*What?*" Lord Dancer leaned forward, his

gorgeous robes hunched about his shoulders, his pale eyes boring into those of the foreman. "*What* did you say?"

"Not proven, my lord."

A great cheer went up from the court. The earl, who did not know the sympathy of the spectators had swung in favour of Maggie, looked wildly at Mr. Farquharson for help.

"What does the verdict mean?" he demanded. "Is she guilty or not?"

"Aye, it's very strange that England and Scotland should share one Court of Appeal — the House of Lords — and one Parliament for so long and yet maintain such different procedures," said Mr. Farquharson. "England has never had a 'not proven' verdict."

"But what . . . ?"

"Oh, it means she goes free. Not proven is a peculiarly Scottish verdict which the cynics translate as either Go away and don't do it again, or We know you're guilty, but we can't prove it."

Maggie was turning her head this way and that as people reached up to seize her hand to congratulate her. Lord Dancer had slumped back in his chair in disgust. Mrs. Chisholm, the wardress on Maggie's right, whispered something in the ear and she gave a wan smile.

Cheering sounded from the mob waiting outside the court.

"Aye, they love her today," sighed Mr. Farquharson, "but by tomorrow the wind will change and they'll always be wondering whether she did it or not. That's the awful thing about a 'not proven' verdict. It doesn't matter where she goes, people will always look at her sideways, and no man in his right mind is going to marry her."

Inside the court, all was chaos. Reporters ran hither and thither, each trying to find out by which door of the court Maggie meant to make her exit.

"I must see her," said the earl, after Maggie had been led from the dock.

"Now, now," said Mr. Farquharson soothingly, "there's no need for that. She'll be well looked after."

But the earl was already off and struggling through the crowd. Mr. Farquharson reflected sadly that he did not really know young Peter very well after all. Why, the man was running after a possible murderess like any other vulgar notoriety-seeker. But Peter Strange was his guest — he could never really think of his young friend as the Earl of Strathairn — and it was his, Mr. Farquharson's, duty to see that no harm came to him. He found the earl after a search. He was in a room off the main court with Maggie Macleod and Mr. Byles, her counsel. Flora Meikle stood sentinel by the doorway.

"I came to collect ye, Lord Strathairn," said Mr. Farquharson, his accent broadening in his embarrassment. He kept his eyes averted from Maggie. "I'm right glad Mistress Macleod is free and it's unco' guid o' ye to concern yourself with her welfare, but, och, I'm sure the lassie has relatives to take care of her."

The earl hesitated. Maggie sat with her eyes downcast. He wished to leave with Mr. Farquharson but found he somehow could not.

Mr. Byles cleared his throat. "I would like you, Mr. Farquharson and Miss Meikle, to wait outside until I have a word with Mrs. Macleod and Lord Strathairn in private."

Mr. Farquharson opened his mouth to protest, but the earl said, "Please leave us," and he reluctantly withdrew from the room, accompanied by Miss Meikle.

Mr. Byles waited to make sure they had gone and then he said, "My lord, this strange marriage of yours has been on my conscience. Provided I do not keep you to it, then there is no reason why it should be considered legal and binding. It is a form of marriage which has all but died out. You are a young man and were no doubt carried away. As you can see, Mrs. Macleod is a free woman and there is nothing to stop her returning to her home and making a new life for herself."

The earl's first reaction was a feeling of intense relief, as if he, too, had just been found not guilty of a crime. He was now free to go back to his happy, carefree bachelor life. Perhaps it was the thought of the life he had experienced since inheriting his peerage — a mixture of loneliness and indolence — that irked him, but much to his surprise he found himself protesting, "I feel it would be ungentlemanly to leave Mrs. Macleod like this. What sort of life awaits here? The verdict did not clear her name. Her home will be surrounded for weeks by photographers and reporters and the curious public. Have you any relatives, Mrs. Macleod? Your father . . . ?"

"I don't know where my father is," she said in a flat voice, drained of all emotion. "I only know that if I did find him, then he would not give me a home. I have no other relatives that I know of.

"I agreed to marry you, my lord, because I felt you had been tricked into it in some way. A bet, perhaps?"

The earl flushed.

"I was sure I would be sentenced to death so it did not seem to matter very much either way." She raised her eyes to the earl's. "As far as I am concerned, my lord, the marriage, if such a comedy can be called a marriage, never took place."

"But what will you do?" demanded the earl.

"I don't know," she said wearily. "I just don't know."

The earl thought quickly. He could not bring himself to walk away and leave her to her fate. That was something the Marquess of Handley would do and Lord Strathairn did not want to be like the marquess. It would do no harm to get her away from Glasgow for a bit, away from the staring crowds. Then, when she had recovered from the murder and the trial, and the interest in her had died down, why, then he could return her home with an easy conscience.

"I, too, agree to forget all about the marriage," he said. "Some day I will explain to you why I behaved in such a foolish and callow manner. I have discovered I own a town house in St. James's in London. Would you like to come to London with me for a bit? Mr. Byles will find a way we can leave the court without anyone seeing us. Say you will come. I promise to take care of you until such time as you are recovered from this nightmare."

She looked at him very steadily and she wondered what he was thinking.

"My lord," said Mr. Byles sternly, "I would like to believe your motives are of the purest, but you must admit . . ."

"My motives are altruistic," said the earl crossly. "I have no interest in Mrs. Macleod as a woman, only as a fellow human being in need of help."

Mr. Byles studied the earl's face. It was too handsome to be trustworthy, he decided, and yet there was a firmness about the jaw and mouth and a steadiness in the earl's gaze which belied the philanderer.

"I think," he said cautiously, "I should leave the decision to Mrs. Macleod."

Maggie turned her steady gaze on Mr. Byles. "Do I have any money?" she asked.

Mr. Byles looked startled. "Where were your wits during the trial, my girl? And, when your late husband's solicitors called to see you in prison? Mr. Macleod left you a great deal of money, not to mention his house and all the contents."

For a brief moment, a vision of escaping to America flashed through Maggie's mind. She was just about to refuse the earl's offer when there came a great, impatient roar from the crowd outside — Maggie, Maggie, *Maggie*. She shivered. She studied the earl with sad eyes. He did not look as if he would beat her. Her father had run her life, then the inspector. It was better to settle for the evil one knew. She was tired, so dreadfully tired. This aristocrat was holding out the promise of an escape to London, away from the jeering crowds, away from the black savagery of this low-country city.

"Very well," she said softly. "I will go with you, my lord."

"I think you should learn to call me 'Peter' and I shall call you 'Maggie'," said the earl, affecting a light-heartedness he did not feel.

But Maggie had turned her head away and appeared lost in her thoughts.

Mr. Byles looked at them doubtfully. "I shall not mention the marriage to anyone," he said. "I will find some means of smuggling you both out of the court. I would advise you both to be discreet and circumspect in your behaviour, or you may both end up having to marry each other properly."

He opened the door and signalled to Mr. Farquharson, who was in the corridor outside, to join them. Flora Meikle remained on guard outside the door.

"Mr. Farquharson," said the earl, unable

to look his old friend in the eye. "I would be grateful if you could send my man, Roshie, here with my bags. Tell him to get me two first class tickets for the London train and, of course, one for himself."

"What's this?" cried Mr. Farquharson. "In the name o' the wee man, you're never going to London with Mistress Macleod!"

All Mr. Byles' doubts were re-animated by the look of shock on Mr. Farquharson's respectable face. "Indeed, I think you have not thought the matter over properly, my lord," he ventured. "But I would like to point out . . ."

"And I would like to point out," said the earl, "that I am thirty-two years of age which is nearly middle-aged. I am neither abducting Mrs. Macleod, nor do I plan to seduce her."

But the earl had only begun to present his case. It was a full hour before he could convince Mr. Farquharson to agree to let him leave the court and go to London with a woman whose name had not been cleared of the charge of murder.

In the days that followed he often thought that had Mr. Farquharson not put up such a staunch opposition to the idea, then he might easily have changed his mind and left Maggie to her fate.

With an enormous belch of black smoke and a high wailing whistle, the *Grand Scotsman* puffed out of Central Station, slowly gathered momentum, and in no time at all was hurtling out of the city of Glasgow, tossing black tenements aside, straining and puffing and panting, clattering over the points, as if desperate to reach the countryside.

The earl leaned his head back against the blue upholstery of a first class compartment and wondered for the first time if he were as mad as Mr. Byles and Mr. Farquharson obviously believed him to be . . . not to mention Roshie who was somewhere further down the train in a second-class compartment.

Their escape from the court had gone off very smoothly. Flora Meikle, acting as decoy, had donned clothes similar to Maggie's and, heavily veiled, had been led from the court by Mr. Byles and into a closed carriage. It was only when she alighted at the Macleod home in Park Terrace and threw back her veil that the Press and the crowd realized they had been tricked.

Opposite the earl, Maggie Macleod had fallen asleep, her face white and strained, even in repose.

Thick eyelashes lay against her wan cheeks

and her mouth looked soft and vulnerable.

The earl sighed and looked out at the flying fields. The round green hills of the southern uplands stretched on either side, dotted with sheep. Great fleecy clouds raced across the sky. The wires on the telegraph poles appeared to fly up and up to join them and then suddenly to be pulled down just when it might seem they would disappear from view. The train gave a long melancholy whistle and plunged into a tunnel. He fingered the little gift-wrapped box on his lap. Roshie had given it to him before they got on the train, saying it was a present from Mr. Farquharson.

As the train hurtled out into the daylight once more, he idly unwrapped it and uncovered a small box. *Parkinson's Miracle Emetic* said the label. "For all cases of poisoning, take two spoonfuls and send for the doctor."

The earl burst out laughing and wrapped the package up again so that Maggie should not see it.

And then he thought, "I don't know whether she did it or not. I'll never know now."

He had been so sure of her innocence in court when everything and everyone seemed to be against her.

But now . . .

The train plunged into another tunnel with a great wailing roar and his fingers tightened involuntarily on the little package in his lap.

Five

It was only when Roshie silently handed him the London newspapers at Euston Station that the earl realized his flight was not going to solve anything unless he took action very quickly.

He had thought the case of Maggie Macleod would only have been featured in the Scottish newspapers. But every London newspaper was full of it.

The earl had not grasped the fact that the 'great' murders, the ones that the public read about avidly and remember for years afterwards are the respectable ones, the ones with a middle-class background.

There were plenty of murders in the teeming slums, but no one paid much attention to them. It took a really solid respectable setting to titillate the imagination of the public. The poor and the aristocracy were expected to sin; the middle classes were not.

The earl stood scowling down at the newspapers, wondering what to do. Maggie would need a chaperone. He had no intention of setting up house with her openly.

But what to do?

He suddenly recalled he had a maiden aunt living in a village in Oxfordshire. He had not seen her for many years but he hoped she was still alive. London was too dangerous. Too many eyes.

Maggie was too tired and numb to protest when she learned their journey was not at an end, and that they were to take the train to Oxford and from there, hire a carriage to take them to the village of Beaton Malden.

She had slept most of the journey but still looked exhausted.

But it was already eleven o'clock at night and Roshie muttered he was sure they would not get a train to Oxford until the morning.

"The house in Charlton Street," said the earl suddenly. "Are there servants in residence?"

"Oh, no, my lord," said Roshie. "The old earl aye took the servants doon frae Scotland. It's a wunner ye didnae ken that," he added tartly.

The earl stared at him coldly for a few moments, reflecting there was a lot to be said for the more obsequious manner of the English servant, but contented himself by asking in a voice of chilling politeness how one got into the house.

"I hae the key," said Roshie. "I carry a spare set o' keys around wi' me to a' your lordship's property."

"Well," said the earl, brightening, "we may as well go there for the night." He turned to Maggie. "We may have to sleep without linen but we'll manage somehow."

"I wish I had a change of clothes," murmured Maggie in her soft voice, her eyes flinching away from the passing crowd since the station was busy even at night.

"We'll arrange something in the morning," said the earl. "We could go to an hotel, of course, but someone might recognize you."

The house in Charlton Street had belonged to the Strathairn family for over a hundred years. It was a prim Georgian building with shallow marble steps leading up to a glossy black door with a fanlight.

On either side of the door were still huge snuffers where the link boys used to extinguish their torches.

Roshie put a large key in the lock and opened the door. His face had not relaxed its lines of disapproval since they had left Glasgow.

"Is there any electricity?" asked Peter, groping about in the blackness of the hall.

"No, my lord."

"Well, light the gas."

"Nae gas, my lord. Just candles."

"Dear God," said the earl impatiently. "Then strike a match, man, and light some candles and take some money and find some restaurant which will supply you with food for all of us."

Roshie muttered something in Gaelic, and the earl sensed rather than saw Maggie's hurt.

"You will speak English from now on, Roshie," said the earl sharply. "Mrs. Macleod is to be treated with courtesy at all times. Do I make myself clear?"

"Yes, my lord," said Roshie gloomily. He lit a candle and led the way into a drawing-room on the ground floor and proceeded to light branches of candles until the room was flooded with a soft light.

Peter looked around with pleasure. The furniture had obviously not been changed since the days of the Regency. Faded, striped, green-and-gold wallpaper adorned the walls and the chairs and tables were Sheraton and Chippendale.

Maggie sank down into a chair beside the cold fireplace.

"Before you go to find that food," said the earl to Roshie, "be a good fellow and see if there's anything to drink in the cellars."

Roshie's face brightened for the first time

101

that day and he hurried off, to return some minutes later with a bottle of whisky and three glasses.

"You may join us for a drink later, Roshie," said the earl firmly. "Food. Now."

"Very well," sighed Roshie, backing out, his eyes fixed longingly on the bottle.

The earl poured two glasses of whisky and gave one to Maggie. Then he bent and put a match to the paper and sticks which were arranged in the hearth and added lumps of coal from a brass scuttle, concentrating on his task until a cheerful blaze was crackling up the chimney.

"Well, Maggie," he said straightening up. "Here we are."

"Yes," said Maggie wearily. She finished her whisky in one gulp and held out her glass for more. Maggie was fortifying herself for the inevitable. Soon they would go to bed and this strange young man would proceed to do all those terrible things to her that Inspector Macleod had done. Why couldn't they all leave her alone? Why was she so weak and spineless? She should have stayed in Glasgow and suffered the curiosity of the mob until the house was sold and then she should have escaped to America . . . alone.

As if to confirm her worst fears, the earl

said, "I'll just take a candle and inspect the bedrooms."

He was gone for some time. Maggie heard the street door bang and the sound of dishes being laid in the dining-room across the hall. There was a great to-ing and fro-ing as if Roshie had brought back the entire staff of a restaurant to cater to his master's needs, which, in fact, was exactly what the enterprising Highlander had done.

At one point, Roshie walked into the drawing-room where Maggie sat and said, "With your permission, Mrs. Macleod," and, without waiting for it, poured himself a liberal glass of whisky and knocked it back in one gulp.

He then gave Maggie a jerky little bow and left the room. His face had been a polite mask, but Maggie knew that Roshie disapproved of her, to say the least.

Dinner was a silent affair. Roshie had banished the restaurant staff before calling Maggie from the drawing-room. He was afraid she might be recognized.

The earl joined Maggie as the soup was being served by Roshie. "We're lucky," he said cheerfully. "I've been quite the little housewife. The beds are made and the fires are lit. Roshie! Splendid man! Where did you conjure up this banquet?"

"Wee place I ken," said Roshie. "The food's no' bad."

"Pull up a chair, Roshie," said Peter. "You may as well join us."

Maggie ate very little and drank quite a lot of wine. She was very silent, and soon the earl stopped trying to make conversation.

"Now, Maggie," said the earl when the silent meal was finished and Roshie had retired to the kitchens with a tray of dishes. "Come and I will show you to your room."

He was surprised by a look of disgust on her face, quickly masked. Nonetheless, she followed him quietly up the narrow staircase with its beautiful thin curving mahogany banister. He pushed open a door. A large four-poster bed dominated the room and a small fire crackled brightly on the hearth.

The earl stood looking down at her. He knew she was frightened and distressed and wanted to say some words of comfort, but he could not begin to guess what she felt. Her drawn, tired face had a tight, withdrawn look.

"Goodnight, Maggie," he said finally. "I shall see you at breakfast."

Her wide brown eyes stared up into his blue ones. Her gaze then flicked from the bed and back to his face and her eyes filled with tears.

"Oh, thank you," she said. *"Thank you!"* And, throwing her arms around his neck, she kissed him on the cheek.

He patted her clumsily on the shoulder and said again that he would see her in the morning. He half turned in the doorway and looked curiously back at her. How incredibly beautiful she looked with her huge peaty eyes shining with gratitude and her midnight-black curls rioting about the creamy pallor of her face and neck!

He raised his hand in a sort of salute and gently closed the door behind him.

Why had she suddenly been so grateful? he mused, as he removed his clothes in the privacy of his room.

All at once he realized she had been afraid that he wished to seduce her. He smiled ruefully as he climbed into bed.

Meanwhile, Maggie undressed in front of the fire. She would need to sleep in her petticoat. Miss Meikle had offered to return from Park Terrace with a suitcase but Mr. Byles had pointed out that she would undoubtedly be followed, and so Maggie had had to board the train without a change of clothes.

There was a tall chest of drawers in one of the shadowy corners of the room, and, after some hesitation, she softly drew open the top drawer.

It contained a few scarves and gloves, smelling faintly of musk. She opened one of the long drawers underneath. There was underwear, yellow with age, wrapped in tissue paper, the lace as fine as cobwebs. She would be able to change her underthings after all, the previous wearer having been as slight as herself.

She selected a nightdress, wondering who had last worn it and how old it was.

She climbed into bed, shutting out thoughts of the trial, of the earl, of her dead husband, firmly from her mind. She could not think of anything. Not yet.

Or she might go mad.

Another train, this time to Oxford.

Maggie, again silent, sat opposite the earl, her face a closed mask.

She had hardly said a thing, except 'yes' or 'no'. He wondered if she had murdered her husband. Of course, he could simply ask her, but the sight of her withdrawn face stopped him. Why was it she had seemed so innocent in the court? Why should he have these terrible doubts now?

As the flat fields of Oxfordshire began to roll past, he decided it was because he did not know her at all. She was a stranger, her very Highland-ness making her foreign to him. Her silence seemed unnatural.

By the time the train steamed into Oxford, he decided her reticence was downright sinister.

As the carriage that they had hired in Oxford took them out towards the village of Beaton Malden, the earl explained that his maiden aunt, a Miss Sarah Rochester, might not still be alive. He had not seen her in ten years. She lived in a large house on the outskirts of the village. And Maggie listened to all this information with apparent indifference.

The carriage at last stopped in front of an old iron gate bearing the legend, *The Laurels*. A short drive led up to the house which was a sprawling, rambling affair of mellow brick, so covered with ivy and creeper and roses that it was hard to guess its age.

"I want you to wait in the carriage, Maggie," said the earl. She nodded her head, taking off her hat and placing it in her lap.

The earl and Roshie left and Maggie sat alone in the carriage, fatigue keeping her thoughts at bay. The air through the open carriage window was gentle and soft. It was almost as warm as a summer's day. Great fleecy clouds sailed high above a pale blue sky, as pale and blue as the eyes of Lord Dancer.

No! Don't think!

After what seemed like a very long time, the earl opened the carriage door. "My aunt will see you now," he said. "She is in the garden."

He led her through the sunny cluttered rooms of the house and out through the french windows at the back. A wrought-iron staircase led down to a pretty garden where a large woman stood by a sundial, waiting for them.

She was dressed in mannish tweeds and wore a hard celluloid collar with a thin black tie. Her pepper-and-salt hair was clubbed short at the neck and she had a great beefy face with wiry grey hairs sprouting from her chin. Her eyes were small and brown and wistful, a contrast to the truculence of her face, making her look like a tired bulldog, dreaming of the days of succulent bones, long gone by.

"So you're Maggie Macleod," boomed Miss Rochester. "Well, what I want to know is . . . if *you* didn't murder your husband, then who did?"

Maggie halted on the bottom step and stared at Miss Rochester. She put a shaking hand to her lips and then fainted dead away.

For the next two weeks, Maggie Macleod lay in the upstairs bedroom at the back of

The Laurels while the doctor came and went. The days grew darker and colder and the birds cheeped dismally in the ivy around the windows. Shadows of leaves flickered across the walls by day, and candlelight sent dark shadows looming out of the corners of the room at night.

Raging with fever, tortured by nightmares, Maggie tossed and turned. At times she felt she was back in bed with her husband and his great body was suffocating her and his coarse voice was muttering obscenities in her ears. At other times, Lord Dancer stood at the end of the bed, slowly raising the black cap and putting it on his wigged head. Sometimes she was back in her father's shop, slicing bacon, cutting cheese, measuring potatoes out of the barrel into the heavy brass scoop, parcelling sugar into blue paper bags and lentils and split peas into brown paper bags, looking up from her work and seeing the shadow of the inspector's thick body falling across the floor of the shop.

One night she looked through the distorted windows of her delirium to where her husband and Murdo Knight sat playing cards at the end of her bed. "This'll make me superintendent," said the inspector. "This'll make me superintendent."

"What will?" cried Maggie desperately, feeling that she must have his answer, but their figures faded and once more she was back in court and Lord Dancer was putting the black cap on his head.

And then as the first snow of the winter began to fall on the ploughed brown fields of Oxfordshire, Maggie's dreams abruptly changed. She had been allowed once during her brief schooling to go on a school picnic to Glen Strathfarrer and in her dream she was back in the cart with the schoolgirls, giggling and laughing while the cart lurched and bumped and the sun slanted through birch and hazel, pine and spruce. A salmon leapt high in the river with a flash of silver scales. In reality, her father had descended on the picnic before it had hardly begun and had dragged her back to the shop, grumbling that he needed help. But in her dream, no angry father appeared and she could smell the tangy scent of pine and bracken mixed with the picnic smells of tea and strawberries.

She opened her eyes to find pale sunlight shining in at the bedroom window and the heavy figure of Miss Rochester sitting reading beside the bed.

"Thank goodness," said Miss Rochester, putting down her book. "I thought you were going to die on me. How do you feel?"

"Strange," murmured Maggie. "Weak."

"Don't try to speak," said Miss Rochester, lowering her normal booming tones with an effort. "I'll just sit here and read."

Maggie closed her eyes and fell asleep again, so deeply and completely that at times Miss Rochester would lean forward anxiously and feel her pulse.

At last, after two hours, Maggie awoke again. She lay quietly watching Miss Rochester's heavy bulldog face bent over her book.

"Where is Peter?" asked Maggie at last.

"Gone to London to see about something," said Miss Rochester, leaning over the bed and straightening Maggie's pillows. "See here, I'm sorry I said that thing about wondering who had really killed your husband. Was that what made you ill?"

"Not really. Well, it was," murmured Maggie. "No. Don't feel guilty. It was just that I had never thought . . . Life seemed so hard and cruel that I almost came to believe I'd done it."

Her voice trailed away. "Don't speak. You're far from well," begged Miss Rochester.

"No, I want to," said Maggie slowly. "I never thought, until you said it, that the murderer of my husband is still at large. You

111

don't know . . . you can't know . . . what it's like. Men. First father, then my husband. Always helpless. Always at their mercy. The murder trial seemed an extension of my life. Cruelty and humiliation. Cruelty and . . ."

Her eyes closed. Miss Rochester leaned forward, but Maggie had fallen asleep again.

Two months drifted past and still the earl did not come. Maggie grew stronger and was able to spend most of the day downstairs.

It seemed that once she had begun to discuss the murder with Miss Rochester, Maggie could not stop. Words poured from her, her soft Highland voice telling Miss Rochester of her life with her husband. Miss Rochester often turned brick red to the tips of her ears. Maggie almost seemed to think her husband's treatment of her was the normal behaviour of a married man, while Miss Rochester shuddered at the sadism revealed in Maggie's gentle narrative.

But Miss Rochester was a great believer in the healing powers of 'getting it all out' and so she listened patiently as Maggie talked and talked. One question kept returning. Who had killed her husband?

"Probably one of those criminal types he met in his job," said Miss Rochester robustly.

"Didn't he discuss his work with you?"

"Never," said Maggie. "I was supposed to stay in my room until he came home at night and then he usually brought Mr. Knight with him. I thought Mr. Knight — that reporter, you know — might have softened my husband's attitude towards me for it was after Mr. Knight started coming that Mr. Macleod suggested I might like to visit the shops and buy things for myself. But then . . . but then, Mr. Knight spoke so cruelly of me at the trial. It sounded as if he were describing another woman. It all seemed so inevitable somehow . . . that I should hang. Men. All those men ranged against me. Lord Strathairn marrying me for some joke." Maggie blushed. "I should not have said that."

"Oh, he told me all about it. But didn't my silly young nephew *tell* you why he asked you to marry him?"

Maggie shook her head.

"Well, I will." Miss Rochester had been planting seedlings in a flower bed beside the cane garden chair on which Maggie was resting. Although it was the beginning of March, the day was pleasantly warm in this sheltered area of the garden. Behind the garden wall, the wind roared through the trees, making a sound like the sea. Miss

113

Rochester leaned back on her heels and told Maggie about the bet with the Marquess of Handley.

"You mustn't think too hardly of Peter," ended Miss Rochester. "Men are funny about bets. They'll cheat their wives and their tailors without a blush, but settle their gambling debts they will, come hell or high water."

"Poor Lord Strathairn," said Maggie. "What will he do? Mr. Byles said he need not consider himself married to me and I shall certainly not hold him to it." Maggie looked across the lawn to where a blackbird was engaged in tugging out a large worm. "I shall soon be strong enough to go home, and then you too will be free of me."

"Nonsense," said Miss Rochester gruffly. "Haven't had such a fascinating thing happen to me in ages. We'll be like Sherlock Holmes and Watson . . . don't know who's who. We'll go back to that godforsaken city and find the culprit."

"No!" said Maggie, involuntarily.

"Not now. Not yet," said Miss Rochester, stooping to her work again. "You'll have to be strong in mind as well as body. I'll stick with you and you tell me when you feel you're ready. Trouble is, you ain't had any fun. Young gels like you should be going to balls and parties and theatres."

Here she twisted her head and looked at Maggie wistfully. "I haven't been to a play in years. Haven't got the money for jaunts to town. But Peter has. We could live at that town house of his for a bit and do the Season."

"I couldn't," gasped Maggie, sitting upright. "People would recognize me and it would be awful for you and Lord Strathairn."

"Tell you a bit about m'self," said Miss Rochester, jabbing the edge of the flower bed viciously with her trowel.

"My father was the dean here, and I gave up my whole life to the church. After mother died, well, it seemed natural that I should fill her shoes, making parish calls, running mothers' meetings, doing the flowers, that sort of thing. And then father died and I was left with this house and a little annuity, enough to live on.

"Before you came, I was thinking of all the things I hadn't done . . . apart from not having married, I mean. I was thinking, I never had any fun. It seems I was born middle-aged, grew up middle-aged, and here I am in my fifties and ought to be content. But all I want is just one fling. Just one. Just to walk down Piccadilly and see the electric lights and see the new motor cars and go to the music hall and eat dinner at midnight, and . . . oh, so many things that people do without thinking.

"I'll see to Peter. We could dye your hair. Give you another name. No one will be looking for Maggie Macleod at the London Season. Please!" Miss Rochester had turned beet-red with excitement and her eyes were as guileless as a child's.

Maggie gave a little sigh and looked about the sunny garden. How lovely it would be to stay here and never have to see anyone in the outside world again. It was the first time in her young life that Maggie Macleod had had the friendship of another woman. It seemed to her that it was the first time anyone had ever been kind to her, anyone had ever wanted to listen to her. And in Maggie's Highland code, kindness must always be repaid, never taken for granted.

"If Lord Strathairn agrees," she said sadly, "then I will go."

Maggie lay back in the cane chair and closed her eyes. She still tired easily. The sun shone through the bare branches of willow tree at the edge of the garden and threw a network of shadows on Maggie's pale face. Miss Rochester, who had opened her mouth to say something, closed it again and fought silently with her conscience.

"I am using the girl," she thought grimly, "because I feel if I don't have one little bit of excitement, I shall go *mad*. But it would do her good as well, so I am not being entirely selfish."

Her young companion had fallen asleep, her face calm and relaxed. The long folds of her teagown moved gently on the grass at her feet, blown by a soft breeze. Miss Rochester had had several gowns made for Maggie by the village dressmakers. They were, she realized, hardly *haute couture*, but what was precisely wrong with them, she couldn't quite say. The materials were of the best. Perhaps it was because they were too fussy.

It would be hard to persuade Peter to allow them to live in Town. He seemed content to send an allowance for Maggie's keep, and seemed to expect the arrangement to go on indefinitely. He had been kept well informed of Maggie's progress back to health but he did not seem to feel any urge to see the girl himself. But Peter had always been a handsome devil, even as a boy. He probably had a lady-love tucked away somewhere in London. Maggie Macleod was beautiful. But Lord Strathairn did not even seem to have noticed.

And then Miss Rochester began to consider her own appearance. She thoughtfully ran her square hand with its stubby fingers across her chin, feeling the wiry length of the long hairs which sprouted so energetically and embarrassingly.

Lord Strathairn climbed slowly down from the rented carriage which had brought him from the station at Oxford, paid the driver and then let himself quietly into *The Laurels*.

He had been busy putting the house in Charlton Street in order, moving down the Scottish servants, and hiring a firm of decorators to restore the old mansion to its former beauty.

For the earl was beginning to grasp the immensity of his fortune. Not only that. He had been helped with his task of decorating by the fascinating Mrs. Murray, a society widow of great wealth and beauty.

An old army friend, on leave in London, had met him at the Cavalry Club and had taken him along to one of Mrs. Murray's afternoon salons. The earl had been charmed and bewitched. Mrs. Murray had appeared delighted with the new earl and had recommended a firm of interior decorators in which she held a controlling interest, although she omitted to tell his lordship that fascinating fact.

Scotland, Maggie and Miss Rochester had been pushed to the back of the earl's mind.

He was calling at Beaton Malden only to make sure that Maggie was fully restored to health. His conscience was easy. He was paying Miss Rochester a generous amount to take care of Maggie. He now had his life neatly mapped out. Maggie should stay with Miss Rochester until she felt well enough to travel north, and, hopefully, out of his life.

At times he wondered what had possessed him to take on the onerous charge of looking after a possible murderess. Mr. Byles had shown him the way out and the girl herself had said she would not hold him to the odd marriage. At times the earl also wondered what had possessed the Marquess of Handley to play such a malicious trick. Possibly the man simply enjoyed the sight of other people's humiliation. Goodness knows, he had met enough of that kind before.

Money was a great healer. He could satisfy himself that he had behaved very generously towards Maggie by supplying her with a companion, a home and the best of medical attention.

He realized he had, in fact, come to say goodbye.

Suddenly an agonizing scream rent the air. And another.

The noise was coming from the bedrooms upstairs.

Heart beating hard, he took the steps two at a time.

Another scream. It was coming from Miss Rochester's bedroom.

He flung open the door of his aunt's bedroom. She was seated at her dressing-table, her face buried in her hands.

"What's the matter?" he cried. "Where's Maggie?"

Miss Rochester raised an embarrassed face which looked strangely red and raw.

"It hurt so," she mumbled. "But I got it all off."

"What the dickens . . . ?"

"My whiskers," said his aunt, blushing a fiery red. "I was using hot wax to take off my whiskers and it hurt like the very devil."

"My dear aunt," said the earl with great relief, "I thought you were being murdered. Such cries of agony! Why all this sudden beautifying?"

Miss Rochester looked at him cautiously. "Tell you later," she mumbled. "Maggie's in the garden."

"I would like to talk to you first," said the earl. "Do you think Maggie was responsible for the death of her husband?"

"How can you *think* such a thing?" Miss Rochester lumbered to her feet and began to pace up and down the room like an agitated elephant, the drooping hem of her teagown trailing along the carpet. "The girl's innocent. As a matter of fact, I've grown very fond of her which is why I have a suggest . . ."

"Splendid!" interrupted the earl. "That is why I am prepared to continue to pay you an allowance so that you can . . ."

"*Suggestion* to make," continued Miss Rochester firmly. "Seems to me that little gel could benefit from some social life. Take her around a few places during the Season."

The earl thought immediately of the beautiful Mrs. Murray. He could not wait to return to London to continue his courtship, for he realized that that is what it was. Courtship. He had surely done enough for Maggie Macleod.

And he said so. He explained at great length that he had decided at last to get married and that he would find the presence of a young lady in his house difficult to explain away.

While he was talking, Miss Rochester's brain was working furiously. All at once she realized she had expected the earl to fall in love with Maggie and live happily ever after. Not for one minute had she envisaged him having the remotest interest in any other female. Now it seemed as if the earl would live in London and she and Maggie would stay in Beaton Maldon and that was that.

Goodbye to glorious dreams of parties and theatres, bustling streets and electric lights — Beaton Maldon was lit by candles, had not even gas, and still boasted the services of an antiquated link boy to light you home at night.

Miss Rochester took a deep breath. "See here, Peter," she said in her gruff voice, "it's all very well to give the girl money and gowns and a home. But money doesn't solve everything. She's all right in body but her mind's still troubled and she's had a quite dreadful life. Wouldn't it be splendid just to give her a few weeks' fun? I would take care of her. Nobody need know who she is. Surely interest in Maggie has faded by now. We could say that she's your cousin. Yes, that's it! No, don't interrupt! Hear me out. We could call her by another name. All you need to do is introduce her to a few young people and I'll do the rest."

"I don't want to seem callous . . ." began the earl.

"Of *course* you don't, Peter. I just *knew*

you would agree." And seeing that he was about to protest, she rushed forward and enveloped him in a great bear hug.

"Aunt Sarah, I . . ."

"And Maggie's in the garden. Do run along and see her, dear boy, while I do something with this old face of mine."

The earl bit his lip. He turned and left his aunt to her beauty aids and went slowly down the stairs, feeling trapped. Why had he visited Beaton Malden? A letter would have sufficed. He simply could not trail around the London Season with a notorious Scottish murderess in tow. "And I'll bet she did murder Macleod," he thought viciously.

He paused at the top of the garden steps leading down into the garden.

Maggie was lying back in a long cane chair, the type they have on cruise ships, reading a book. Her hair was tied at her neck with a pale blue ribbon, and one long, airy tendril floated against the faint healthy pink of her cheek. As if she sensed him standing there, she put down her book and looked up. Her eyes widened slightly and she gave a hesitant smile.

The earl walked down the steps towards her. It was her very reactions to him that were strange, he thought. He was used to girls simpering and flirting and blushing, always the awareness in their eyes that he was a marriageable man.

But this girl with her wide, wary eyes viewed him as she viewed most people, with a hint of timid fear. "Please don't get up," he said as she would have risen to her feet. He drew up one of those heavy garden chairs which are described as 'rustic', all uncomfortable knots and bumps, and sat down next to her.

The garden blazed with a sort of ordered jumble of spring flowers although the air still retained some of the cold of winter.

"How are you?" asked the earl, wondering all the while whether he would always have this nagging doubt about her, always wonder whether she had killed her husband.

"Very well, thank you my lord."

"Peter."

"Peter, then," smiled Maggie shyly.

Maggie had forgotten how very handsome the earl was with his crisp gold hair and strong, tanned face. His eyes were extremely blue and fringed with heavy lashes. He was wearing a blazer and flannels with a soft white shirt and cravat.

"Miss Rochester has outlined a plan to me," said the earl. "She thinks it would be a good idea if you came back to London with me. She feels that your mental health would benefit from a little social life. We have decided that you should change your name and we will put it about that you are a cousin of mine." The earl watched her covertly as he spoke, hoping she would refuse.

Maggie sat silently, her eyes veiled. Another man in her life, another house to be shared. He had been very patient, but surely once they were both living under the same roof he would expect some sort of reward? Maggie had a sudden memory of the inspector's sweating, grunting body and shivered.

She became aware that the earl was still speaking.

"Of course," he was saying, "I can't promise to be always on hand to squire you about. The fact is . . . as a matter of fact, I . . . dash it all, I want to get married."

"To me?" asked Maggie wonderingly.

"Well, no. Not you. You very kindly said you would not consider that silly business in Glasgow legal and binding. I have met a perfectly splendid lady."

Maggie's first feeling was one of relief. But that feeling was immediately followed by a sense of loss, tinged with depression.

She glanced at the earl from under her lashes. The sun was gilding his crisp hair. His long, strong hands were clasped around one knee and he was watching her anxiously.

Maggie did not think much of herself. All at once it seemed natural to her that such a very good-looking man as this earl should not find her attractive in the least. He belonged to another world. A golden sunny world where young people laughed and flirted and fell in love. She wished he would go away and leave her in this quiet country village with Miss Rochester. But Miss Rochester wanted one last fling and without Maggie's co-operation she would not get it.

"I should like to go to London for a little," she said in hesitant, soft voice. His face became a social mask but she knew he was disappointed and that he had been hoping she would refuse.

Sympathy for his predicament made her ask softly, "This lady, is she very beautiful?"

"Very," smiled the earl. He tried to conjure up a picture of Mrs. Murray in his mind, but her image seemed to be blotted out by the presence of this girl with her disturbing, haunting beauty. So, instead, he remembered Dolly Murray's sparkling, witty, frivolous conversations which always made him feel exhilarated, as if he had been drinking champagne. He could never imagine Maggie saying anything frivolous and the thought made him smile again.

"She has brown, glossy hair," said the earl, "and a very trim figure. But her great charm is in her manner. She is very witty and gay and all the chaps adore her. I'll be very lucky if she accepts me."

"Is she very young?" asked Maggie, trying to overcome her natural shyness in an effort to please him.

"Yes. No. Well, not as young as you. Mrs. Murray is a widow."

"Oh, and what happened to Mr. Murray?"

The earl gave a light laugh. "As a matter of fact, I forgot to ask. It's not the sort of thing one does ask, like, say, 'What on earth did you do with Mr. Murray?'. Oh dear," he added guiltily as Maggie flushed. "I forgot. You're a widow as well."

"I think," said Maggie, carefully changing the subject, "that Miss Rochester intends to take me about. There will surely be no need for you to escort us. I would not wish to spoil your courtship."

"Oh, I don't mind taking you around a bit," said Peter, relaxing as he realized that Maggie did not mean to maintain any hold over him, or to insist they were married or anything awkward like that. "You'll need some good clothes. Good heavens! Where did you get that gown?"

"Is there something wrong with it?" asked

127

Maggie, fingering the fine lace of her gown. "Miss Rochester had it made by the village dressmaker. It's quite the nicest thing I've ever worn."

"Won't do," said the earl severely. He looked at the satin frills and bows that embellished the bodice. "It's too *bunchy.* You should wear simple, elegant lines. Mrs. Murray wears beautiful clothes. When she drives in the Park, people stand on chairs just to get a look at her."

Maggie fought down an irrational feeling of dislike for this Merry Widow and said, "Oh," in a small voice.

After a little silence, Maggie asked, "Did you bring Roshie with you?"

"No, I left him in London. Why?"

Maggie gave a little sigh. "I fear he does not approve of me."

"Roshie is sometimes too outspoken," said the earl. "What did he say to you? That night when we first arrived in London and he spoke in Gaelic?"

"It does not matter," said Maggie. "I would not be wanting to get the man into trouble."

"I insist."

"Oh, dear. Well, he said, when you mentioned getting the food, that he hoped there wouldn't be any poison in it."

"That's more than enough," said the earl wrathfully. "He has gone too far."

"You must not be angry with him on my account," said Maggie. "Roshie is very loyal to you and he simply thought you were making a mistake. There's more than Roshie will think so."

"There's no need for anyone to find out who you are as long as you are in the south of England," he said, thrusting his hands into his trouser pockets and stretching out his long legs. "Why does Roshie have a different accent from you? He's Highland as well, isn't he?"

"He's from Argyll," explained Maggie. "Their English is a little broader than ours in the north and they speak Scots as well as the Gaelic; they use quite a lot of words in the dialect. Now me, I hardly used English at all when I worked in my father's shop. We spoke the Gaelic at home. I'm used to the English speech now, but at first I was that slow for I had to translate what people were saying into Gaelic in my mind, answer them in my mind in the Gaelic, and then translate it back into English."

"Do you miss your home? The Highlands, I mean. Not Glasgow."

"Not really," said Maggie, twisting a fold of her gown between her fingers. "I think my father treated me badly. He would not have been able to marry me off to Mr. Macleod, perhaps, if I had gone to Lord Lovat."

"Who is Lord Lovat? Oh, of course, I know. He owns all the land around Beauly. But what difference could he possibly have made to your father's arrangements?"

"Well, you should know," said Maggie in slow surprise, "being a lord yourself. Lord Lovat sees to the welfare of all his tenants, and if you have a problem — och, about anything — his lordship will aye sort it out."

"But surely if one's tenants are well-housed and fed, one need not concern oneself with the problems of their family lives?"

"Oh, well," sighed Maggie, "you're English, so I suppose it's different. They haven't the heart in them. Like the Duke of Sutherland. He was English and he had the people driven out of their houses to make way for sheep. They were given seven days to get out and if they didn't, the factors would burn the roofs over their heads. But Lord Lovat is not like that. He was away at the time Mr. Macleod arrived and I had never got to know anyone in the town very well, and the ones that I did know slightly were all afraid of my father."

"And would Lord Lovat have interested himself in the marriage of a young girl?"

"Perhaps," said Maggie. "Perhaps."

"But," the earl burst out, "surely he leaves someone in charge?"

"That's not the same. A man working for his lordship would not be concerning himself with our little troubles. Nor should he. We are not his people and it is not his land."

"Dear me. Are all the Scottish aristocracy so patriarchal?"

"The good ones. Yet, of course, there are bad ones."

"Like me."

"Now, I did not say that," said Maggie with a rippling laugh.

The earl drew out a flat silver case and extracted a cheroot. He lit it and blew a cloud of smoke into the air.

Perhaps there was more to this business of being an earl than he had realized. He felt obscurely guilty. He had not paid much attention to the people in his county after he had noted that they all seemed relatively comfortable and prosperous.

He thought of Mrs. Murray and wished she were with him now. She would surely tease him out of these burgeoning scruples. He thought of Mrs. Murray at Strathairn and wondered if the tenants would like her, and, in almost the same moment, decided he was being ridiculous. It did not matter whether they liked her or not.

He wanted to forget about Scotland. Scotland meant the gloomy tedium of Strathairn Castle and the grim, black tenements of Glasgow and his taking on that stupid bet. He did not wish to think of Scotland. Let them all go to the devil. But he could not get rid of that nagging feeling of guilt and decided, unfairly, it was all Maggie's fault.

He cast a sour look at Maggie who was smoothing a fold in her dress. What did she think when that vague, dreamy look crossed her face?

He did not like women with an air of mystery. Leave all that sort of rubbish to willowy aesthetes. He liked his women pretty and jolly.

Miss Rochester was surprised on descending to the garden half an hour later to find that the earl had gone. Maggie told her that he had said he would send for both of them at the end of the following week.

Maggie looked sad and had faint purple shadows under her eyes.

"Did he tell you about that woman he wants to marry?" asked Miss Rochester anxiously.

"Yes, he did that," said Maggie wearily. "A widow, she is. A Mrs. Murray."

"I *never* trust widows," snapped Miss

Rochester, stumping off to order dinner and quite forgetting that her young guest was a singularly notorious member of that despised species.

Six

Three weeks had passed since their encounter in the garden, and somehow Maggie Macleod was still making the earl feel guilty. Not that she was Maggie Macleod any more. She was Miss Margaret Dunglass, a relative who had been sent to London to 'do' the Season.

The earl sat in Mrs. Murray's elegant drawing-room and thought some dark thoughts about Maggie. She and Mrs. Murray had not yet met, although Mrs. Murray never seemed to tire of asking the earl questions about his mysterious cousin.

The earl would laugh and say Margaret Dunglass was a quiet little thing, very retiring, and Mrs. Murray would look pleased and drop the subject, only to return to it a few days later. For Mrs. Murray had begun to think this cousin was a very bad influence on the open-handed earl.

Perhaps she had reason to.

It had all started when Maggie had arrived at the house in Charlton Street. She had eyed the bright new William Morris wallpaper and the new sea-green carpet and the *art nouveau* hangings, and, when pressed for an opinion, had said that it had looked more 'homey' before, and the earl, who was reluctantly inclined to be of the same opinion but did not want any criticism, even several times removed, of his beloved Dolly Murray, had become quite angry with her and had said caustically that Maggie herself could do with being 'done over' since her clothes were 'homey' to say the least.

He had not seen much of Maggie and Miss Rochester after they had moved in. Miss Rochester had plunged into a hectic round of innocent London life, dragging Maggie around all the sights, to all the playhouses, and for long, energetic walks in the parks.

Then, only that morning, the bill had arrived from the firm of interior decorators. He had been shocked at the price and had said as much in Maggie's hearing. The girl had quietly taken the bill from him, studied it carefully, and then had said calmly that he was being 'robbed blind'.

Fortified by this remark, the earl had duly so far forgotten himself as to tell Mrs. Murray that he was being robbed blind by the interior decorating company.

Now Mrs. Murray was walking up and

down her drawing-room, trying to control her temper. "What do you plan to do about it?" she asked at last.

"Nothing, personally, that is," said the earl, and then, quoting Maggie, he added, "There's nothing in that bill that cannot be sorted out by a good firm of Scottish lawyers."

Mrs. Murray glared at him in alarm. His Scottish lawyers would soon find her own name on the books.

Forcing a smile, she sat down on the sofa beside him and gazed into his eyes. "Dear Peter," she murmured, "you are becoming *so* Scotch, counting every penny. It is not at all the thing to quibble over such matters. If you hire the *best*, then you must pay for the best. Please say you will let the matter drop. After all, I recommended the firm, and I would certainly not, had I guessed you were going to be so . . . so . . . *parsimonious*."

Her little dimpled hands flew to her face and she gave a choked sob.

"Mrs. Murray. Dolly," said the earl, gently drawing her hands away from her face. "You are quite right. I am being such a bear."

"You've never been the same since that cousin of yours arrived," sniffed Dolly.

"Oh, don't let's talk about her," said the earl. "Let's talk about us. Are you coming

136

with me to the opera tonight?"

"Darling Peter, I can't. I've got to see this dreary aunt in Surrey."

"Must you? You did promise to come."

"How frightful. So I did. But Auntie is due to pop off at any moment and the old thing won't leave me her goodies in her will if I'm not at the bedside to clutch her scrawny hand. Why don't you take that little Scotch cousin and your aunt whatsername?"

"Aunt Sarah? Yes, that might be an idea. If you can't come, then I don't really care who I take along."

"Darling flirt," she murmured. She moved away from him a little and asked lightly, "Is there another lady in your life? Mrs. Jouffrey says she saw you in Asprey's, picking out a divine diamond necklace."

The earl carefully studied the toe of his elastic-sided boot. Mrs. Murray had hinted often and delicately that she adored diamonds. He had at last taken the hint and had bought her a magnificent necklace at Asprey's. He had taken it home and had shown it to Maggie and Miss Rochester.

Maggie Macleod had stared at the necklace and had said in soft surprise, "I thought Mrs. Murray was a lady!"

"Of course she is," the earl had snapped.

"I didn't think you gave ladies that kind of

present until you were engaged to be married," Maggie had said seriously. "You see, Miss Rochester's teaching me a lot about etiquette."

"Etiquette! Aunt Sarah, you have some very antiquated notions."

"Really!" Miss Rochester had barked, shifting her great bulk uneasily on a spindly chair. "That sort of thing hasn't changed, let me tell you. Propose first, necklace afterwards. I mean, she didn't *ask* for diamonds, did she? Only a tart does that."

And so the earl had decided that, of course, Dolly hadn't asked or even hinted and had put the necklace away in his bureau drawer.

"Oh, that," said the earl, smiling at Dolly Murray. "I didn't buy it," he lied. "I like looking at diamonds because they remind me of you. Sparkling and shining and very, very precious."

Dolly Murray looked at him thoughtfully. Surely Maria Jouffrey had said the earl had *bought* the necklace. To hint again that he should buy her a little token of his affection was too blatant. Especially since she was sure he meant to marry her. But why didn't he *ask?*

She did not know that the earl was pursuing an old-fashioned course of courtship.

One courted during the Season and proposed at the end of it. Dolly had many admirers but she had gradually discouraged them all with the exception of the earl. Could that mysterious cousin have something to do with his reluctance to propose?

She glanced at him from under her eyelashes. "Do you think your cousin will catch a fellow this Season?"

"I don't think she wants one," said the earl before he could stop himself.

"No girl is *that* divorced from humanity. What does she do? I haven't seen her in the Park or at Ascot or Henley or any of the balls."

"She and my aunt have been sightseeing. I haven't seen much of either of them. Perhaps I will take both of them to the opera tonight. I have a box."

"You simply must bring Miss Dunglass to one of my salons."

"Who?"

"Your cousin."

"Oh, yes, of course. I mean, I don't think she would accept. Very retiring sort of girl. We always end up talking about her. Let's talk about you, Dolly." He smiled into her eyes and Dolly smiled back, not really seeing the earl but only the Strathairn fortune.

★ ★ ★

Miss Rochester was thrown into quite a flutter by the invitation to the opera. To date, she had carefully concealed her disappointment in the earl, for he had not offered to take them anywhere at all, and although she was enjoying an innocent sort of day-trippers' London life, with visits to Madame Tussaud's and the Tower and places like that, it did seem irritating to be perpetually *out* of society when one's host was *in*.

Most of the new gowns she and Maggie had ordered had been delivered just that day. Miss Rochester was clever enough to know that she had no dress sense whatsoever and had put them both in the willing hands of Madame Vernée, a modiste with a clever eye for line and colour. Her bills were staggering but Miss Rochester had naïvely assumed that since the earl seemed prepared to pay that ridiculous decorator's bill, then he would hardly quibble at the expense of a few gowns and mantles.

Maggie, too, was flustered by the unexpected invitation. Unlike Miss Rochester, she did not long to venture into society. She had thoroughly enjoyed the outings with her new friend, and Westminster Abbey and the Tower of London were more suited to her unsophisticated tastes than any grand ball or party.

She had resigned herself to the fact that the earl would shortly announce his engagement to Mrs. Murray. Mrs. Murray must be very charming and beautiful, thought Maggie wistfully.

Maggie felt the earl had been very kind to her and wondered that she had ever thought him a wild young man who enjoyed proposing marriage to accused murderesses in order to satisfy some decadent need.

Sometimes in the privacy of her bedroom, Maggie could not help wishing that life had been different and that she were in fact married to the earl, but she quickly suppressed these thoughts, putting them down to vanity. The earl was rich and handsome. But she wasn't in love with him and so it was wicked to even think of marriage. Maggie had only recently begun to read novels again and it seemed quite logical to her now that one only married for love, and that to find that luxury you had to be high-born. Why else would all these novels only deal with the yearnings of Lady This and Lord That? For people of her own degree, there was only lust followed by child-bearing.

That evening, as he waited downstairs in the drawing-room, the Earl of Strathairn

141

smiled wryly at his own snobbery. It would have been fun to go to the opera with the dazzling and chic Dolly Murray on his arm instead of two ladies who would undoubtedly be dressed in the worst of provincial taste.

He had no fear of meeting the Marquess of Handley, Lord Robey or Alistair Ashton. To his request for news of these gentlemen, his chamberlain at Strathairn had informed him that the marquess was in Deauville and the other two were safely tucked away on their estates.

Miss Rochester was the first to enter the drawing-room and the earl looked at her with surprised appreciation.

Nothing could be done to make Miss Rochester look beautiful but she did look magnificent in an imposing way. She was wearing a modish gown of claret-coloured satin, cut low to reveal a surprisingly white pair of shoulders. Her pepper-and-salt hair had been piled high on her head and frizzled at the front to disguise her knobbly forehead. Artificial claret-coloured silk roses were threaded in her hair and she carried a magnificent osprey fan with diamonded sticks. She minced forward on the unaccustomed height of a pair of French heels and looked at the earl timidly.

"I don't look an old fright, do I?"

The earl handed her a glass of sherry. "You look marvellous," he said. "All the young fellows will be fighting to take you away from me."

Miss Rochester gave a girlish giggle. "Wait till you see Maggie, and you won't even look at me," she crowed.

"Nobody could outshine you this evening," said the earl quietly. "You've been hiding your light under a bushel all these years."

"I'm glad it's worth it," said Miss Rochester. "My corset is killing me."

The earl grinned and then turned as the door of the drawing-room opened and Maggie Macleod walked in.

He stood looking at her in absolute amazement while Miss Rochester watched him gleefully.

Maggie was dressed in a gown of pale lilac chiffon which seemed to have been moulded to her figure. The skirt was caught up at the back into a bustle and layer upon layer of scalloped chiffon cascaded down to form a short train. Her shoulders rose from the tight bodice, white and soft and feminine.

Her glossy hair was piled up on her small head in an intricate arrangement of gleaming curls. Her eyes were very wide and dark in the exquisite oval of her face. The only make-up she wore was a little rouge on her lips. She carried a black lace fan and a heavy green and gold opera cloak over one arm.

Maggie looked at the earl nervously. He was staring at her in such an odd way. He was wearing faultless evening dress with a scarlet-lined opera cloak, fastened with a gold chain, slung around his shoulders.

"I know what you need, Maggie," he said suddenly, and quickly left the room.

"What's the matter?" asked Maggie nervously. "Doesn't he like my gown?"

"Oh, he likes it all right," said Miss Rochester cheerfully. "I wonder what he's doing."

In a few moments the earl was back, carrying a flat morocco leather box. He opened it and lifted out the necklace he had bought for Mrs. Murray and said to Maggie, "Turn around."

"Oh, those are for Mrs. Murray!" cried Maggie, looking thoroughly upset.

"Well, I agree I shouldn't give Mrs. Murray expensive presents until we are engaged," said the earl lightly. "But there is nothing to stop me giving them to my cousin."

"Do as he says and let him put the things on," urged Miss Rochester. "You need some jewels."

Maggie meekly turned around and the earl clasped the diamond necklace about her neck. She trembled slightly as his hands touched her skin.

Roshie came in to announce the carriage was waiting and stared at the vision that was Maggie Macleod.

"Michty me!" exclaimed Roshie. "Ye look like a princess."

The earl held out one arm to Maggie and the other to his aunt. Strange the workings of fashion, mused Maggie, that even Roshie should look at her without his customary disapproval.

It was as well, the earl thought, that Maggie was so totally and completely engrossed in the performance of her first opera. She was quite unaware that she had created a sensation from the moment she had arrived at the Royal Opera House, Covent Garden. Men and women alike jostled each other aside to get a better look.

When the opera, *Rigoletto*, began, Maggie leaned forward slightly, her lips parted, engrossed in the music. Miss Rochester immediately fell asleep.

The earl was all at once aware of Maggie's nearness. She was wearing a delicate, subtle perfume unlike the heady musky scents Dolly Murray wore. He had certainly been aware before that Maggie was a pretty girl. It was only this evening that he realized she was beautiful. It was not only her appearance but her air of soft femininity and the way she seemed to sway slightly as she walked.

Disloyally, he felt that Dolly Murray would have been all too aware of the admiration and would have paid little attention to the music, waiting only for the interval so that she could be 'on stage' with her crowd of admirers.

He reminded himself severely that he was in love with Dolly, intended to marry her, and that this fair charmer beside him had probably put arsenic in her husband's tea.

He glanced at Maggie sideways, at the beautiful shape of her mouth and wondered what it would be like to kiss her, to place his hands on those perfect breasts, cunningly revealed by the tight chiffon bodice of her gown. He tried to fight his thoughts which were becoming increasingly erotic, putting them down to the darkness and intimacy of the opera box and to the enchantment of the soaring music.

The earl longed for the interval when the lights would go on and Maggie Macleod would revert back to the little Highland girl he had brought south from Glasgow, instead of this disturbing enchantress whose skin gleamed like pearl in the darkness of the box and whose perfume was doing exciting things to his senses.

But when the lights went up and Miss Rochester slept on, Maggie turned and faced him, a drowned look in her eyes, and said simply, "I did not think there was anything so beautiful in the whole world."

"Neither did I," said the earl quietly, but he was not talking about the music.

As the opera went on and the Duke taunted and Rigoletto plotted revenge, the earl envied Maggie her absorption in the music. Her silk-gloved hands lay in her lap and he had a longing to stretch out and take one of her hands in his. He remembered how ill she had been and how he had called in the best doctor he could find and then how he had escaped to London. How could he ever have left her?

"Steady, boy," he admonished himself.

"It's a trick of the music. You love Dolly Murray, dammit. You can't fall in and out of love like this. The minute you see Dolly again it will be all right."

He was to see Dolly again sooner than he knew.

Mrs. Murray had visited her aunt, had held her hand, and had talked about the sheer Christian goodness of making a will.

147

But her aunt had fallen into a deep sleep in the middle of this interesting monologue, leaving Dolly bored and restless. She glanced at the watch pinned to her bosom. Eight o'clock. All at once she decided to return to London. She would have time to change and be at the opera for the final curtain. That way she would get a glimpse of this mysterious cousin of Peter's.

The earl descended the stairs of the opera house with Maggie on his arm, stopping to introduce her to some of his new friends, noting the jealousy in the women's eyes and the hunger in those of the men.

Maggie smiled prettily and said little. Miss Rochester was yawning horribly and muttering that opera always sent her to sleep.

And then, he saw Dolly Murray standing at the bottom of the stairs. She looked handsome, sparkling and bright, her glossy brown curls swept up under a magnificent tiara of diamonds and rubies. Her black and rose-pink striped gown was daringly cut. Her eyes, which had looked at the earl with such roguish tenderness, now held a steely glint as they fastened on the necklace of diamonds glittering against the white skin of Maggie's bosom.

The earl made the introductions, and Maggie smiled at the other woman and said warmly, "I am so glad to meet you at last. Peter has told me such a lot about you."

"Indeed!" Dolly gave a brittle little laugh. "I mean, how frightfully *odd*. He has told me absolutely *nothing* about you. But that's my Peter for you. You must come to one of my salons and meet some of my *younger* gentlemen friends, although darling Peter is so possessive, I think he has frightened most of them away. You know Sir Percy Blythe, don't you?"

The earl nodded and introduced Dolly's escort to Maggie. Sir Percy was a young man with a great waxed moustache and ingenuous hazel eyes. "By Jove!" he said, seizing Maggie's hand and pumping it up and down. "You're the most beautiful thing I've ever seen." He had moved close to Maggie as he spoke and she blushed with embarrassment and recoiled a little. The earl put a protective arm around her shoulders, caught the startled look in Dolly's eyes, and hurriedly withdrew it.

Dolly had every reason to look surprised. Gentlemen and ladies did not touch in public, no matter how intimate they might be in private. Putting your arm around a woman at the opera was tantamount to a proposal of marriage.

Dolly decided the sooner she broke up

149

this little gathering, the better. She was clever enough to know that she was appearing at a disadvantage beside this cousin.

"Call on me tomorrow, Peter," murmured Dolly, giving him an intimate smile. "Come, Percy."

Percy, who had been staring open-mouthed at Maggie, gave himself a shake like a dog and led Mrs. Murray away.

Dolly Murray burned with rage and jealousy. She realized it was not only the Strathairn fortune she wanted to get her hands on, but Peter himself. He had looked so distinguished and handsome tonight, and . . . "They make a splendid couple, Strathairn and Miss Dunglass," said Sir Percy brightly.

"You make my head ache," snapped Dolly. "Stop goggling at me like a stuffed cod and take me home."

Maggie and the earl were very quiet as the carriage bearing them back to Charlton Street swung around into the Strand. The earl tugged down the window letting in a wave of warm night air with its smell of hot pies, cigar smoke and patchouli.

Miss Rochester wondered if they had quarrelled but she was too sleepy to care, and, when they arrived home, she excused herself, muttering to Maggie that all she wanted to do was get off her corsets and have a good scratch.

The earl felt suddenly restless, his thoughts confused. "I want to walk," he said suddenly. "I don't think I can sleep."

"Neither can I," said Maggie softly. Her glittering evening had somehow fallen in ruins about her feet the minute she had seen the hard, accusing eyes of Dolly Murray.

"Come with me," said the earl. "We'll walk until we're tired."

Maggie nodded as if the suggestion of a walk around the London streets at midnight was the most natural thing in the world. "I'll change into something more suitable," she said, unclasping the necklace and handing it to him.

"Keep it," said the earl harshly. "I wish I'd never seen the bloody thing."

"I'll put it away and give it to you in the morning," said Maggie quietly. "Are you jealous of Sir Percy?"

"Good heavens, no!" said the earl in great surprise. "Should I be?"

Maggie did not answer, merely repeating that she had better go and change. Her Scottish maid, Betty, was waiting up for her and pestered her mistress with questions about the opera. Betty had been brought down with the other servants from Scotland as parlourmaid and had been elevated to the position of lady's maid when Miss Rochester and Maggie had arrived from Beaton Malden. Apart from Roshie, not one of the other servants had recognized Maggie Macleod in the quiet Miss Dunglass.

Maggie answered as many of Betty's eager questions as she could and then sent her off, saying she would put herself to bed. She felt it would be too exhausting to try to explain to Betty why she was about to change and go out walking in the middle of the night with Lord Strathairn, since she did not herself know why she was doing it.

She changed into a tailored skirt and a high-collared lace blouse and put on a tight little black felt jacket.

She pinned on one of the new 'pancake' hats which had arrived from the milliner that day and tilted it forward on her forehead, pinning her curls into a *chignon* at the back. Quickly working the buttonhook with nimble fingers, she donned a pair of kid boots, marvelling that boots should be so fine and elegant, and then ran lightly down the stairs and into the drawing-room.

The earl had changed into a venerable blazer, a relic of his Balliol College days, and a pair of grey flannels.

They walked through the quiet streets of

St. James's and down to Pall Mall, then past the black Tudor bulk of St. James's Palace, along Trafalgar Square, down Northumberland Avenue and along the Embankment where the huge round moons of the lamps sent their shadows scurrying behind them into the darkness. A few lights shone in the factories on the Surrey side, sending their reflections twinkling on the dirty, sluggish waters of the Thames.

"Has Sir Percy known Mrs. Murray long?" asked Maggie, breaking a long silence as they stood with their elbows on the balustrade and watched the moving river. Big Ben sounded one o'clock, one long harsh chime.

"Percy? I don't know. She knows a lot of men."

"How old is Mrs. Murray?"

"Dolly? About the same age as I, I suppose. About thirty-two."

"As old as *that!*" exclaimed Maggie, making the earl feel like Methuselah. "She is a remarkably fine-looking woman."

"Yes." The earl shifted restlessly. He had hoped to walk away from this new enchantment Maggie held for him, but she seemed even more vulnerable and feminine in her walking dress than she had done in her opera gown.

"Tell me about your husband," he said.

153

"I don't want to talk about him," said Maggie quickly. "Please don't ask me anything about the murder. It haunts my dreams. I want to be Margaret Dunglass tonight . . . your cousin and your friend."

He was strangely touched. "Very well, Miss Dunglass. Do you feel tired?"

"Not in the slightest."

"Then, Miss Dunglass, we will walk to Covent Garden and buy hot coffee from the stall and put the world to rights. What do you want to talk about?" he went on, taking her arm and leading her away from the river.

"Nothing serious," said Maggie. "Nothing that concerns *now*. Tell me about the books you've read and the places you've seen. Roshie said you had been in India. I know, tell me about that."

And so the earl talked about his regimental life, of tiger hunts, of monsoon weather, of heat and death and strange Indian customs. He lost himself in his memories, reliving old scenes and old battles, dimly aware that Maggie was losing herself in his stories, both of them living in his past to block out the present with its long shadows of murder.

They drank coffee, standing amid the debris of old programmes and oyster shells in Covent Garden. Then they strolled back to the Thames and across the bridge to Waterloo Station.

"Let's go somewhere," said the earl, looking at the list of places chalked on the departure board. "Let's just pick out a place and go there."

He did not want the night to end, to sleep and wake to the reality of an angry and jealous Dolly Murray and the fears that he might be keeping a murderess under his roof.

"Look at that," Maggie laughed, and he thought he had never before seen her so young and carefree. "Bennington-Super-Crash. There can't be such a place."

"There must be," smiled the earl. "Let's go and see."

There was a milk train leaving in fifteen minutes' time so he purchased first-class tickets and the morning papers and they steamed out of Waterloo Station as the sleepy pigeons began to come awake and the sky turned to light grey.

The train chugged its lethargic way through the buildings of London and out into the English countryside. A large red sun rose above the fields, slowly changing to gold, and flooding the frowsty compartment with warmth. Maggie felt sleep pricking at her eyelids and determinedly fought it off. To go to sleep would mean the end of the dream. The train picked up speed and fussed energetically past trees and hedges, letting out an occasional squawk of a whistle blast.

At last it slowed and rattled over the points and came to a stop with a series of spasmodic lurches.

"Bennington-Super-Crash," called a hoarse voice from the platform.

"We're here," said the earl, "and just in time for breakfast. I'm starving."

They climbed down onto the wooden platform and watched while the train gave a cough, a belch of black smoke and chuffed busily away.

They handed their tickets to a sleepy ticket collector and walked out into a small station yard ablaze with geraniums.

It was very quiet and still, the only sound in the silence the clopping of the milkman's horse. The road from the station wound down into a picturesque village. Thatched cottages crouched along the edge of a wide village green where story-book ducks bobbed on a round pond and a brown Jersey cow studied its reflection in the water.

At the end of the village stood an old posting-inn called *The Barley Mow*. It had a thatched roof, white walls, green shutters, and roses round the door.

"Incredible!" murmured the earl. "I expect mine host to come bustling out wearing a powdered wig. He will have a large stomach hanging over his knee breeches. It's all so perfect. Perhaps not a landlord. I know, a plump, motherly matron with a print dress smelling of lavender and wearing a huge starched apron. Her cheeks will be rosy, her eyes welcoming, and her hair shining with silver threads."

They stepped into the small entrance hall of the inn, so small there was only room for a table, a hatstand and a brass bowl with a glossy aspidistra.

He rang a brass bell on the hall table, looking at it with distaste as he did so. It represented a simpering lady in a crinoline.

The landlady came sweeping out and Maggie stifled a giggle. She was tall and angular and dressed in black silk covered with a quantity of cameo brooches. Her sallow face was set in lines of permanent disapproval.

"You're very early, sir, madam," she said.

Maggie felt like apologizing and saying they would come back later, but the earl said breezily, "What on earth is the Crash?"

"It's the river, I mean the River Crash," said the landlady, startled. "It flows at the bottom of the inn garden."

"Splendid!" said the earl. "Let's go and have a look at it."

The landlady opened her mouth to protest and then closed it again and reluctantly led the way through the inn parlour, through a dining-room at the back, and out into a garden which consisted of some rustic tables and chairs, a sloping lawn and some lovely old trees.

The River Crash flowed silently at the foot of the garden, a moving mirror of lazy blue water with flag iris standing sentinel at the edge and a scarlet rowing boat shifting gently on the movement of the stream.

"Beautiful," said the earl, stretching his arms above his head. "Simply beautiful. Gosh, I'm hungry!"

The landlady pursed her lips. "It is a little early for breakfast, sir, but . . ."

"Breakfast! Who wants breakfast?" laughed the earl. "By Jove, we haven't even had supper. Get us a champagne supper and pack it up and we'll take that boat along the river and have a picnic."

"Really, sir," began the landlady. "I . . ."

"And plenty of rugs and cushions," added the earl cheerfully. "Come along, Maggie. We'll sit and watch the river until it's ready."

He turned his back on the landlady and led Maggie to a table near the water's edge.

How wonderful to have that sort of confidence, thought Maggie. He's never paused for a minute to think the landlady might not want to do it, and so he will probably get what he wants.

And that is exactly what happened. In no time at all, an ostler and a boots were carrying out a large hamper down to the boat, followed by a housemaid, carrying rugs and cushions. The landlady did not reappear.

The earl tipped the servants after he had paid the bill and then assisted Maggie into the boat. He picked up the oars and began to row down the stream while Maggie let her hand trail in the water and wished life could always be like this.

Screaming swallows skimmed and dipped over the river, a fish plopped in the lazy warm silence and cattle grazed on the cool green fields which ran down to the water's edge. Thrushes and blackbirds hopped busily on dew-soaked fields and a pigeon was cooing monotonously from a belt of woodland. Far away came the whistle and the shuffling clank of a goods train.

"I think we'll moor over there," said the earl at last. "There" was a semicircle of grass at the water's edge, ringed with trees of birch and larch.

He pulled the boat up on the bank and

then spread the rugs and cushions on the grass and opened up the hamper.

"What have we here? Chicken and rolls and a veal-and-ham pie and a rather limp salad. Champagne, and chilled too! Eat up, Miss Dunglass, before you fall asleep."

So Maggie ate and sipped champagne, feeling the sun warm on her head. She removed her velvet jacket and her hat, and the earl took off his blazer, hung it on a branch and rolled up his shirt sleeves.

After they had eaten, he neatly packed away the remains of the food and plates. Maggie lay on her back, her head against the cushions, and stared up at the shifting pattern of the translucent young leaves. She felt a confused mixture of weariness and exhilaration.

The champagne seemed to be bubbling along her veins. She closed her eyes, feeling the warm sun on her face as it filtered down through the leaves.

The high-boned neck of her blouse was digging into her chin and she unfastened the small buttons at her throat, letting the gentle breeze play on her neck.

She sensed the earl was very near her and opened her eyes. He was lying beside her on a rug, leaning on one elbow and looking intently at her face.

"What's the matter?" asked Maggie sleepily.

"You," he said huskily. "Only you."

Her eyes widened and she stared up into his blue ones which were now so very near her own.

She opened her mouth to say something but her voice seemed to catch in her throat and her lips trembled.

He bent his head and placed his lips very gently against her own. Maggie lay very still, passive, frightened.

He drew back a little and smiled down at her. "Do not be so afraid. I am kissing Miss Dunglass. I know Mrs. Macleod would not approve but then she is not with us. You must kiss me back, Miss Margaret Dunglass. It is only polite."

She gave a weak smile and shook her head, moving her head against the pillows, watching, fascinated, the hard line of his mouth, the faint gold stubble on his tanned chin, and the way the breeze lifted his gold hair on his forehead.

"Then you are going to be very much in my debt, Miss Dunglass," he whispered, "for I am going to kiss you again."

This time he drew her close in his arms and, cradling her head on his shoulder, he bent his mouth to hers again. His lips were

161

warm and exploring, pressing deeper, moving sensuously against her own. Maggie felt a melting, drugged sweetness stealing over her body, a lazy lethargy induced by the sun, the champagne, and the feel of his mouth and arms.

Suddenly she wound her arms around him, digging her fingers into the crisp golden hair at the nape of his neck, and kissed him back on a wave of great all-consuming passion.

His lips moved slowly from her mouth to the sun-warmed skin at her neck where her blouse lay open. She timidly kissed his ear and he gave a low groan and began kissing her breasts which were thrust up by her corset against the thin silk of her blouse.

"Morning, guv," called a cheery voice. "Lovely day for it."

The earl abruptly released Maggie and sat up, his face flaming with embarrassment. An old man was sitting in a rowing-boat in the middle of the river, leaning on his oars and beaming at them.

"Lovely day for what?" demanded the earl acidly.

"Why, for a picnic to be sure," said the old man cheerfully. "Morning, guv, mum." He touched his forelock and began to row energetically upstream.

Maggie had buttoned up her blouse and was sitting, as if turned to stone, staring at the stream.

The earl muttered something under his breath and began to carry the hamper towards the boat. Her silence and stillness made him feel awkward, and he maintained an air of forced jollity as he rowed them both back to the inn.

Dark clouds were moving in from the west, the effects of the champagne were gradually receding, and he was wondering what had come over him. If he did not mean to marry Maggie properly — and he most certainly did not —then he had behaved disgracefully by making love to her, particularly when the girl was a guest under his roof. As he helped her from the boat in front of the inn, she looked briefly up into his eyes, her own dark and shadowed. What did he really know of this girl? The long shadow of unsolved murder laid its cold fingers on his senses.

Her lips opened. She murmured something which sounded like, "You think I did it," but a sudden gust of wind whipped through the old trees about the inn, and he could not be sure he had heard her aright: did not want to know.

There was a silent, weary wait for the next

train. After a few remarks about the weather and the prettiness of the town, the earl found he could not think of another thing to say.

At last the small, busy little train puffed into the station and they climbed aboard.

Maggie felt sleepy and bewildered, the whole episode by the river beginning to appear in her mind like some highly-coloured intoxicated dream.

Before the train arrived at Waterloo, she awoke with a start and saw that the earl was asleep. His face looked grim in repose as if he were regretting his love-making even as he slept.

A thin, greasy drizzle was falling on London when the pair returned to Charlton Street to be faced by the alarmed cries and questions of Miss Rochester. Maggie silently removed herself to her bedroom, and the earl parried Miss Rochester's questions as best he could. Yes, he should have left a note. Yes, he realized he should not have kept Maggie out all night, but they had been restless and had gone for a walk. No, he did not intend to stand all morning answering stupid questions when his head ached like the devil.

He was relieved when a livened footman supplied a welcome interruption by arriving with a note for him.

His relief was short-lived when he discovered the note was from Dolly Murray, issuing a rather peremptory summons that the earl be present at her salon that afternoon.

Seven

The earl was somewhat relieved to find that Dolly's salon was quite crowded when he arrived. There was a new addition to Mrs. Murray's court in the shape of a young niece, Hester Jenkins, who had come to stay.

Hester was, in Dolly's opinion, a country mouse who would no doubt be perpetually awed and grateful that her sophisticated aunt had given her house room for the Season. She was a tall, pale, thin girl with large pale eyes and sensitive-looking hands which belied the fact that she had not one sensitive bone in her body. Hester prized honesty above all things and Dolly had not yet discovered that Hester had a disastrous way of saying exactly what was on her mind.

To Dolly's fury, Hester, in the earl's hearing, proceeded to introduce her aunt to a fine example of this embarrassing trait.

Dolly had been patronizing Hester and remarking that "her little country mouse" had quite terribly antiquated clothes and that she, Dolly, was going to supply her with a suitable wardrobe. "Clothes are so important, I think," remarked Dolly, complacently adjusting the priceless lace ruffles on the bertha of her blouse.

Hester's pale eyes surveyed her aunt, and then she said with dreadful clarity, "I agree. Clothes are very, very important, particularly when one is no longer young. I admire the great effort and hard work you put into your appearance, Aunt."

And when Dolly was reeling from that remark, Hester turned her attention to the room.

Dolly had inherited the house from a relative, and, like quite a lot of rich people, she did not see any reason to spend unnecessary money. She urged all and sundry to redecorate their homes — especially as there was a good chance they might use her decorating firm — while leaving her own, frozen in time, exactly as it had been when her relative had been alive.

It was very much in the style of thirty years ago. There was just too much of everything. Too much carved mahogany and ormolu; too much red, green, yellow and purple plush, and too much patterned velvet; too much gilt; too many laced antimacassars, ribbons and bows. The dyes of the last century were harsh and the colours of the fabrics clashed like cymbals.

Ornamentation trailed writhing and curling over everything. The furniture was heavy and grotesque. The room was filled with endless *bijouterie* and bric-à-brac, loaded whatnots, mirrors framed in plush and then limmed over with birds and flowers. The overmantels of the fireplaces were encrusted with sea-shells. There were pompoms and tassels and fringes; a wealth of mother-of-pearl; jars of potpourri; vases filled with bulrushes and peacocks' feathers; bulbous glass cases enshrining flowers made of wax, or made of dyed feathers or fish bones. And the crowning horror, on the mantelpiece was a nubile marble nymph with a gilt clock stuck in her stomach.

Hester's cold, calm eyes ranged over this tremendous clutter and she said, "I wonder you do not throw out at least three-quarters of this stuff since you do not like antiquated things . . ."

"It has a certain period charm," interrupted Dolly savagely.

"Really? I would not have thought it old enough to be described as period," said Hester thoughtfully.

"Do have some tea, Peter," interposed Dolly desperately.

"It's a wonder," pursued Hester, "that

you don't call in that firm of interior decorators that you own . . . or rather that you have a controlling interest in . . ."

"Hester!" said Dolly sharply. "You are talking nonsense! I am sure no one is interested in . . ."

"Oh, but I *am*," said the earl sweetly. "Two lumps, please, Dolly. You did not tell me that . . ."

"It's not true," cried Dolly.

"There is no need to kick me under the table, Aunt," said Hester. "Also, it is wicked to tell lies. Mama told me all about the decorating firm and about how clever you were to get all those people in London to use it. You should be proud of your business acumen, Aunt," said Hester righteously.

Dolly rose abruptly with a rustling of taffeta petticoats. "The Earl of Strathairn wishes to talk to me in private, Hester."

"Oh, is *that* who you are?" asked Hester, her large eyes swivelling around to fix themselves on the earl. "Did she really poison her husband?"

The earl felt as if the bottom had just dropped out of his stomach.

"I think you said you wanted to speak to me in private, Dolly," he said desperately. He found his arm clasped in a strong grip and looked down into the eager, wrinkled face of Mrs. Jouffrey. "What is Hester talking about?" she demanded, waving a roguish finger under the earl's nose.

"If you will just allow me . . ." The earl tried to pull his arm away. Everyone had stopped talking and Hester's next words carried round the overstuffed room with the clarity of a bell.

"I never forget a face," she said. "Mama has a friend in Glasgow who sent us the Scottish papers. That was Maggie Macleod, the poisoner, with you at Waterloo Station today."

"By Jove," said Sir Percy. "Now I know where I'd seen that face before. That was her at the opera t'other night."

To the earl the room seemed to be full of eyes, staring, accusing eyes. Social ruin stared him in the face, a thing he had not stopped to consider when he had taken Maggie under his wing.

"Well, Peter?" demanded Dolly Murray shrilly. "We're waiting."

The earl's head swam with fatigue. All he wanted to do was get away.

So that is exactly what he did. He simply walked out of the room.

Dolly Murray sat very still, hardly hearing the exclamations and questions and babble of shocked voices. She could say goodbye to the Strathairn fortune. But . . . there was always a little money to be made from the newspapers . . .

The earl erupted into the house in Charlton Street like a volcano, calling for Roshie, shouting orders that everything must be set in motion for a return to Scotland.

And where was Miss Rochester and Miss Dunglass?

Roshie said he thought the ladies had gone to the *Daily Bioscope* in Bishopsgate.

The earl ran out of the house and grabbed the first hansom, lifting the trap of the roof with his cane and calling to the driver to take him to Bishopsgate. Unless he moved very quickly, he suspected his home would shortly be besieged by reporters.

He wondered why Maggie had not simply gone to bed, forgetting Miss Rochester's passion for novelty. The first "cinema theatre" had attracted a lot of attention.

When he arrived at the Bioscope, the show was in progress, and he realized the impossibility of searching in the blackness of the theatre for the two women, and so he took a seat in the back row and waited impatiently for it to end.

Well, there was one thing, the earl decided, this new cinema fad would never replace the theatre. He had never seen anything more boring. Men and women strutted like mechanical dolls over flickering grey scenes where an eternal rain seemed to be falling and box-shaped carriages and automobiles tore around at an insane speed.

At last it was over, and, after fretting and fuming at the exit, he saw Maggie and Miss Rochester, arm in arm. In a low voice he told them that Maggie had been recognized. They must leave for Scotland immediately.

"We'll need to wait until tomorrow," said Miss Rochester in a practical voice.

"No trains until then. We'd better find somewhere to stay the night, outside the town. And we'd better take the North-Eastern Express to Edinburgh, instead of the North-Western to Glasgow for they'll be looking for us on that."

For Maggie, the nightmare had closed in again. She had enjoyed the novelty of the bioscope, and she had enjoyed sitting in the warm darkness remembering the feel of the earl's lips against her own. She had conjured up a rosy dream that they would return home and that he would fall on one knee and say he loved her. But one look at his worried, tight-lipped face banished all dreams.

He was a man chaperoning a possible murderess and well aware of the fact.

From then on, to Maggie, life whirled around in black and grey clouds of despair, lit by occasional flashes of pure fear. What would become of her? Once in Scotland, would Peter send her away? And Miss Rochester? That lady looked as grim and tense as the earl.

There was a hurried dash to Charlton Street, then an escape with only two of the servants — Roshie and the lady's maid, Betty — to an hotel in St. Albans. After a dream-racked night's sleep, off to King's Cross Station, this time to catch the ten o'clock 'Thunderer' which boasted a journey of only eight and a half hours to Edinburgh — and that covered a stop at York for early dinner.

Roshie had bought an armful of newspapers for his master, but the earl, after glancing over the front pages, had opened the window of the carriage as the train was steaming out of the sooty glass cavern of King's Cross and had thrown the lot out onto the line.

A glance had been enough to show him that Mrs. Dolly Murray had talked to about every newspaper in town.

It was a grim, silent journey. The earl was aware that his servants, travelling on the western line, would know by now the real identity of Miss Dunglass.

He had always prided himself on the fact that he did not care for the opinion of others. It was humiliating to find out that he *did* care and that he was no better than anyone else. He felt he was being socially damned as the helpmate of a murderess.

Maggie slept most of the journey. She was heavily veiled. She raised her veil only when they shared a silent dinner at York.

Then there was the arrival in Edinburgh, the train to Glasgow, and the carriage to Strathairn. Gusty sheets of rain were blowing across the park when they arrived at Strathairn Castle.

Despite his distress, the earl experienced a feeling of homecoming, a feeling of safety. The rooms were as heavily carpeted and over-furnished as Mrs. Murray's salon, but everything was well-cared for and loved, the furniture being polished to a high shine and fires crackling on the hearths. Not by the flicker of an eyelid did the well-trained staff betray they knew Maggie's identity.

They had finished a late supper and were sitting wearily in the drawing-room, all aware that the hour was two in the morning, but all reluctant to go to bed. They had conversed in a desultory manner, talking about everything and anything but the murder. The earl did not know what his feelings for

Maggie now were. He only knew that the episode on the River Crash seemed like a small sunlit cameo in his mind, something delightful that had happened to two other people, a very long time ago.

The sudden thudding of the great brass knocker on the castle door made them jump.

"The wind," said Miss Rochester wearily. "Only the wind. No one can be calling at this hour and in this weather."

The knocking sounded again.

"There *is* someone at the door," said the earl, rising to his feet. "I sent the servants to bed so I'd better go and answer it myself."

"Don't go," said Maggie softly. Her eyes held a strange withdrawn look.

"Of course, I'll have to go," said the earl irritably, his nerves almost at snapping point.

He left the room and Miss Rochester looked at Maggie. Maggie was sitting very still, her hands holding onto the arms of the chair, her knuckles white.

"I hope it isn't reporters," said Miss Rochester. "Don't look so strange, Maggie. We all need some sleep."

The drawing-room door opened and the earl entered followed by two men.

"May I present Chief Superintendent John Menzies of the Glasgow C.I.D. and Inspector Henderson," he said in a harsh voice. "They want to see you, Maggie."

The two men advanced into the room. Mr. Menzies was a large burly man with a great spade-like beard and small round eyes like a teddy bear. His inspector was small and wiry with long, drooping side whiskers, and dull green eyes, the colour of Iona marble.

"But it's all over," bleated Miss Rochester. "What on earth do you want to see her about?"

"Well, Madame," said Mr. Menzies, "we just have a few questions to ask the lady so if ye don't mind . . ."

"But I *do* mind," said Miss Rochester, suddenly angry. "I mind very much. It is two in the morning. *Two in the morning.* State the true nature of your business and leave!"

"Very well," said Mr. Menzies. "Mr. Murdo Knight was found at six o'clock this evening in his home in Bath Street, dead as a doornail. It looks as if he'd been killed wi' a big dose o' some poison, probably arsenic. We'll find out for sure in the morning when the Procurator Fiscal puts in his report. The doctor who examined him estimates he died around four o'clock in the afternoon.

"So the question is this, Mrs. Macleod. Where were you at four o'clock yesterday afternoon?"

"I'll answer that," said the earl, suddenly looking much younger than he had done since they left London.

"Mrs. Macleod was with Miss Rochester and myself on the 'Thunderer' bound for Edinburgh. At four-thirty, we had dinner at York in the Station Hotel with about one hundred people as witnesses. So Maggie Macleod could not possibly have been in Glasgow poisoning Mr. Knight. So you'll need to look elsewhere for the murderer of Mr. Murdo Knight, and while you're at it," added the earl with a sudden light-hearted laugh, "you may as well look for the real murderer of Inspector Macleod . . . because it looks as if he . . . or she . . . is still at large."

"Is this true?" asked the Chief Superintendent, swinging around and confronting Maggie. "Were you on that train?"

She was looking straight at the earl, her eyes like stars.

"Oh, yes," she said in her soft voice. "It is indeed the very truth."

By the time she awoke the following morning all Maggie's feelings of happiness had gone.

The earl might think her innocent, but he did not love her. And Maggie loved him. Completely. This shattering thought was the first thing that entered her brain when her eyes opened to the dismal light of a leaden day.

For the first time she was hit by the full impact of how the earl's partisanship must affect him. He would be socially ostracized. Mrs. Murray would not favour him with her smiles again. No society woman worth her salt would marry him solely for his money if it meant she would never be able to show off the clothes and jewels his fortune could buy her.

"But *I* would marry him," thought Maggie, "but he is not of my class, and although he may be kind to me, he would never think of wedding anyone of my station. I am nothing but a shopkeeper's daughter. Only think how they sneered at people in London who were in trade and said they 'smelled of the shop'. I am a woman whose name has not been cleared of the charge of murder."

Her eyes roamed around the solid luxury of her bedroom. The steel bars of the grate shone like silver and the brass scuttle and fire irons like gold. Firelight winked on the deep red depths of polished mahogany surfaces; on the enormous carved bed and on the gigantic wardrobe which reached almost to the ceiling. Heavy brocade curtains had been drawn back to let in the morning light which filtered whitely through fringed and bobbled blinds and under curtains of net.

The mantelpiece was draped with heavy brocade and crowded with china figurines.

What would the servants think of her now that they knew her identity? She sat up nervously as the maid, Betty, entered the room and started laying out her mistress's clothes for the day, placing the underwear on the guard rail of the fire to warm.

But Betty seemed very much her usual self, chattering nineteen to the dozen, brisk and efficient.

Maggie settled back against the pillows with a little sigh of relief.

It was as well for her peace of mind that she did not know of all the excitement raging in the servants' hall.

The butler, Mr. Adams, had started writing his memoirs, "My Days in Service with A Famous Poisoner"; the cook, Mrs. Murdoch, had told the gardener to make sure all cans of arsenic in the potting shed had been thrown away in case "Mrs. Macleod might be tempted"; and the rest of the staff were wondering if selling their story to the newspapers would compensate for a subsequent life of unemployment.

The reporters and photographers were being held at bay outside the gates by two of the keepers armed with game rifles.

The earl had awakened in a worried mood as well. The feeling of elation he had experienced on proving that Maggie was with him at the time of Murdo Knight's murder had faded. Surely this did not automatically prove Maggie innocent. But Knight had been a crime reporter. Perhaps some criminal had put an end to him.

It did not follow that his death was related in any way to that of Macleod. He found Maggie's very manner alien. If she had openly wept and perpetually and vehemently protested her innocence, it would be more in line with what he would have expected any woman to do in the circumstances. Her frequent silences, the way she often dropped her eyes when he looked at her, all suggested something unfathomable and secretive.

Then there were his own feelings towards Maggie Macleod to consider. He may as well admit that she roused violent and very earthy passions in him and the earl felt obscurely that no lady should do that.

He shook his head as if to clear it and came to the conclusion that somewhere in Glasgow the real murderer of Inspector Macleod must exist, and therefore must be found. He might often wonder what Maggie really thought of him, but that no longer

180

made him think her a murderess. Somehow, he must succeed where the whole of the Glasgow police had so far failed.

Still gnawing at the problem, he wandered abstractedly down the stairs and entered the breakfast room. Miss Rochester was already there, toying moodily with toast and tea, great purple patches under her eyes making her look more like a bulldog than ever.

The earl felt a stab of compunction. This whole business, this scandal, was too much for a maiden lady like his aunt. He was just opening his mouth to suggest that she might like to go home to Beaton Malden after she had rested from her journey, when, to his extreme irritation, the butler announced, "Colonel Delaney, my lord," and ushered a small, dapper gentleman into the room before the earl had time to protest.

Colonel Delaney was a well-preserved man in his sixties with a neat round face and neat round figure. He had sparse grey hair brushed over a pink scalp, a thin moustache over a pursed babyish mouth, and shrewd little black eyes. He wore a short fawn coat over tweed trousers and carried a brown bowler and a pair of lemon kid gloves in one hand.

"Good to see you," he said breezily. "I'm Delaney, your neighbour. Thought you might need some help with those scribe-chappies who're baying at your door."

"Sit down and have some tea or coffee," said the earl, privately wishing the colonel in hell. "If you mean the Press, I've got two fellows keeping them off with shotguns."

"Ah, but that's just the point," exclaimed the colonel. "Oh, I do beg your pardon, Madam. We have not been introduced."

His little black eyes twinkled at Miss Rochester. The earl testily introduced him and then sat fuming as the colonel helped himself to grilled kidneys from the sideboard and sat down at the table, obviously determined to eat a hearty breakfast.

"It's like this," said the colonel, waving a kidney speared on the end of his fork. "If you keep 'em out, then all they'll do is pester your servants and tenants and write a lot of distorted muck about you and Mrs. Macleod."

"*But* if you treat 'em nice, why, they'll maybe help find out who really did it, since I don't suppose Mrs. Macleod did for a minute. Now, did she?" He beamed at Miss Rochester with ingenuous charm.

Before anyone could reply, Maggie herself entered the room and there was a small disturbance while the colonel was introduced.

"As I was saying," he went on as soon as Maggie was seated, "the best thing you can

182

do is to have the lads up to the castle, shut them in a cosy room with a lot of whisky and sandwiches, and then give them a rousing speech about how you are fighting to clear Mrs. Macleod's fair name with the help of the free and fearless Press of Scotland. Great stuff! I can see the headlines now: 'The Earl of Strathairn Battles to Clear Maggie Macleod's Name'.

"So with your permission, I'll run out and get these chappies in out the cold. Beastly summer, isn't it? You can give them something nice to write.

"Now you," he went on, picking up Miss Rochester's hand and giving it a playful little shake, "look like a sensible woman to me. I think it's important people should know you are here as well, by way of chaperone."

"I don't think . . ." began the earl, half bewildered, half amused.

"Well, it's time you did," said the colonel cheerfully. "See you in a jiffy. Finish my breakfast after I've got the Press rounded up."

And with that he strode from the room.

"Isn't he marvellous!" sighed Miss Rochester.

"He's rather overbearing," said the earl. "Perhaps he's mad."

"He is talking sense," said Maggie. "Only think how angry the reporters must be. It's beginning to rain."

"I suppose so," said the earl with a reluctant smile. "But he makes me feel as if I've been hit with a whirlwind. Who is this Colonel Delaney, Adams?"

"A retired army gentleman," said the butler, turning from the sideboard. "He has the old manor house about ten miles to the west, just outside the village of Troon. He's well-respected in these parts."

The earl walked to the window and stared out. Through the driving rain he could see a small army of bedraggled men marching up the long drive, shepherded by the colonel.

"What on earth am I going to say to them?" he asked, swinging around.

"Just tell them the truth," said Miss Rochester, tucking into her breakfast with a sudden renewal of appetite.

Soon there was a shuffling in the hall. Adams had sent two footmen to light a fire in the study and a message to the kitchen to send up plates of sandwiches.

The colonel came striding into the room, rubbing his hands. "Well, that's that," he said. "Leave 'em until they've had a few glasses and you'll find them in a mellow mood. They get resentful, you know, when

184

folks don't speak to them. By Jove, isn't this exciting! We have a mystery to solve, so after these gentlemen of the Press have asked all their questions, I'll ask a few. See here," he went on, "the way I see it is this. Murdo Knight is, or rather was, a crime reporter. Mr. Macleod was a police inspector. Together they may have unearthed something that somebody wanted kept quiet. Now, someone poisoned the inspector, but what of Mr. Knight? Suppose he was being paid to keep his mouth shut and got greedy. Hey! How's that for an idea?"

"I think we should leave the detecting to the police," said the earl acidly. He was a little annoyed at the way the colonel appeared to have taken over his home and his life.

"Oh, I wouldn't do that, laddie," said the colonel with unimpaired cheerfulness. "Wouldn't do that, I mean, look at the mess they've made of things already. Do you know that they didn't even use that fingerprint business on the cup on Mr. Macleod's desk? I was interested you see, so I asked a lot of questions. They've been using that fingerprint stuff since eighteen ninety-six, so it's not as if it's brand new. They thought about it, mind you, three days after the inspector died, but by that time the cup had been washed clean and put away with the others. Now what kind of detecting is that, I ask you?"

"Why are you so sure I didn't do it?" asked Maggie.

"Oh, I'm a good judge of character," said the colonel. "I was in the court, you know, and you had innocence written all over you. Now, there's a gel, I thought to myself, who just hasn't the sort of brains to commit a really good murder. Well, now, my lord, I think the jackals will be ready for you."

The earl had an impulse to put him down, to say that he would do as he pleased in his own house and that it did not please him to expose his private life to the vulgar gaze of a lot of newspapermen. But, on the other hand, everything the colonel had said seemed to make sense.

"Very well," he said, and added sweetly, "*Do* make yourself at home, Colonel Delaney."

"Oh, I shall, dear boy," said the colonel. "What a splendid morning! Excellent breakfast and the company of two pretty ladies."

The earl said something that sounded like "tcha" and strode from the room.

Adams was waiting for him in the hall. "The Press persons are in the study, my lord," he murmured gloomily.

"Very good, Adams," said the earl, feeling as if he were a schoolboy again, standing outside the headmaster's study door.

When he entered the room, he was faced by the oddest set of fellows he thought he had ever seen. They came in all shapes and sizes from huge tweedy eccentrics to depressed little men like insurance clerks, to tall willowy men in velvet jackets and Bohemian ties. They rose at his entrance, hanging firmly onto their whisky glasses.

The earl took a deep breath. "Well, gentlemen," he said lightly, "it's a miserable day, and I suggest we all have another glass of something and I'll answer all your questions."

Beaming smiles greeted this. Stories were being rapidly changed around in various minds from, "sinister earl" to "brave earl".

"I wonder how he's getting on," said Colonel Delaney. "I say, is that kedgeree, Miss Rochester? It is! Splendid! I'll have some of that."

Miss Rochester watched the colonel eat with the fond smile of a mother watching her favourite child make a hearty meal.

"I think you should tell Colonel Delaney the whole thing, Maggie," said Miss Rochester, putting down her knife and fork. "It's such a relief to meet someone forthright who wants to help us."

"Lord Strathairn has already been most helpful," said Maggie blushing. "He has suffered so much over his championship of me."

"But he is too close," said Miss Rochester earnestly. "We need a new mind, a fresh look at the problem. Colonel Delaney does not have all the facts. He doesn't even know about the marriage . . ." She broke off and bit her lip in confusion.

"Marriage?" said the colonel, pricking up his ears. "What marriage?"

"I don't know if I should talk about it," said Maggie slowly. "Not without Lord Strathairn's permission. We did not know you until this morning, Colonel."

"But you already feel you've known me for years," said the colonel. "People feel like that about me," he added, stating it as a matter of fact rather than a boast. "You'd better tell me all about it. Mark my words, I think you silly young things have been getting yourselves into a rare old mess." He appeared to include Miss Rochester in his "silly young things" remark and she blushed with pleasure.

"Oh, go *on*, Maggie," she urged. "I'll tell Peter you told the colonel and he won't mind."

Maggie took a deep breath. The colonel was watching her, his twinkling eyes looking infinitely kind. "I'll tell you," she said, her voice ending in a little sigh.

There was a long silence while she marshalled her thoughts. A gust of wind threw raindrops against the window panes and the grandfather clock in the corner sonorously ticked away the minutes.

At last Maggie began to speak, her soft lilting voice telling everything but her love for the earl.

She described her marriage to the inspector, the visits from Murdo Knight, her marriage to the earl, and how the earl had told Miss Rochester, and how Miss Rochester had in turn told her about the Marquess of Handley's bet.

"Well, well, well," said Colonel Delaney, dabbing at his pursed little mouth with his napkin. "It's obvious there's a tie-up somewhere. Why would Handley go out of his way to make such a bet and then see that it was carried through? Unless, of course, he's one of those decadent creatures who humiliate their fellow man for the sheer pleasure of it. And you say that Lord Robey and Mr. Ashton were present at this game? Good. I know them both. Weak but harmless. Ah, I hear a noise. His lordship must be finished with the gentlemen of the Press."

The earl popped his head around the door. "Look here, Maggie," he said. "They want a photograph of you. Do you think you can bear it? They're really not bad fellows."

Maggie hesitated and her eyes flew to Colonel Delaney. She already trusted him. The telling of her story to such a fascinated and sympathetic listener had made her feel as if a weight had been lifted from her shoulders.

"It's all right," said that gentleman. "I'm an interfering old busybody, my dear. But it would be best if you saw them. Don't say much. Just look the way you do now. Bewildered and innocent."

Maggie smiled and moved towards the door. The earl found himself wishing she would smile more.

Her eyes lit up with a deep radiance like the sun on a Scottish loch.

"They're in the study," he said. "Chin up."

He took her hand and raised it fleetingly to his lips. Then he tucked her arm through his and led her from the room. He glanced down at her out of the corner of one blue eye. Maggie Macleod looked every inch a lady, he reflected. She was wearing a fine wool jacket and a tailored skirt in a dull gold colour with a pale, leaf-green blouse with a high-boned collar.

Maggie flinched as they entered the study. All those staring curious eyes reminded her of her trial. The earl pressed her arm and she felt a warm glow spreading through her body.

There was a rattling of tripods and a shaking of magnesium powder.

She stood patiently beside the earl while magnesium flashes burst in her face and shutters clicked and anxious faces peered around black cloths exhorting her to "hold that pose".

What an age it seemed to take one photograph! One dedicated photographer kept talking earnestly about twenty second exposures and began to count, "One Mississippi two Mississippi . . ." while Maggie and the earl waited, feeling the smiles freezing on their faces.

The reporters, while they were waiting for her, much softened by the earl's hospitality and charm of manner, had elected the eldest of them to ask the questions, thereby saving her from having voices shouting at her from all over the room.

He was a large, florid man in an Inverness cape. His red-veined watery blue eyes looked kind enough as he began to question her.

"Tell me, Mrs. Macleod," he said. "How do you feel about all this now? And do you often wonder who really murdered your husband?"

There was a silence while they all waited. The earl looked anxiously down at Maggie and opened his mouth to answer for her. But all of a sudden she began to speak.

"I wonder a lot," said Maggie, her clear, soft voice carrying round the room. "At first I was too dazed and ill." Her voice grew stronger. "But with the help of the Earl of Strathairn, Colonel Delaney and Miss Rochester, I feel sure that the true criminal will be brought to justice. I am well aware now of the integrity of the Scottish Press. I have been told you gentlemen are hard-working and fearless. May you succeed in your efforts." Her voice shook. "God bless you!"

There was a sympathetic clearing of throats.

"Well, she played that one very well," the earl found himself thinking cynically. "Laid it on with a trowel, and just look how they're eating it all up. Cunning little minx. I'll never understand her. Who would have thought she would be so crafty. My God! Maybe she *did* kill her huband. I'll never be sure."

But he let none of his thoughts show on his face.

"Aye," said the chief reporter, writing

busily. "I feel ye cannae have much faith in the police."

"Och, no!" said Maggie, startled. "What else could they think, but that I was guilty? There was so much evidence against me."

She bit her lip and stared at the faces confronting her and her expressive eyes slowly filled with horror.

"The evidence," she whispered. "I've never thought of it until now. That woman who looked like me who bought the arsenic. Someone wanted me to hang for it. Oh, dear God, help me!"

"Curtain. Lights," thought the earl.

She buried her face in her hands. The Press made sympathetic noises while they scribbled gleefully in their notebooks. This was sensation! This was jam! They were a hard-bitten lot, inured to tragedy. Too often they met with rebuffs from the people they were trying to interview. But the Earl of Strathairn and Maggie Macleod had posed for photographs and had given them a story that would make their dour editors sit up and take notice.

And so, in their hearts, they decided Maggie Macleod was not guilty, and each one began to dream of the marvellous story which would surely follow when the real murderer was unmasked.

They clustered around, eager for more, asking questions about Murdo Knight and his friendship with Inspector Macleod.

Colonel Delaney popped into the room. "Enough, gentlemen!" he cried. "Let Mrs. Macleod have a rest. I'll take over now. Have another dram and write up your notes by the fire, and then I feel sure you would like to get back to town."

The earl drew Maggie out into the hall and closed the study door. "I'm beginning to like Delaney," he said. "A bit bumptious, but he seems to know what he's doing. Are you all right?" he asked, as Maggie swayed a little. He put a comforting arm about her shoulders and for one brief moment Maggie allowed herself the luxury of leaning against him. "Yes," she said. "They were much kinder than I expected." She smiled up at the earl and her smile slowly faded. He had an odd expression on his face. His eyes looked hard, calculating.

"Did I say something wrong?" she asked anxiously.

The earl removed his arm and thrust his hands into his pockets. "Oh, no," he said. "You did splendidly. A marvellous performance."

"I was not giving a performance," said Maggie, pink colour rushing into her cheeks.

"Oh, my dear, dear girl! All that cods-wallop about the fearless gentlemen of the Press."

"I meant it," said Maggie, clenching her fists at her sides. "They were so much kinder than I had expected."

The love of her life still had a nasty, cynical look in his eyes, but he shrugged and pushed open the door of the breakfast room.

Miss Rochester looked at them anxiously. A couple had left the room and now two antagonists had returned.

"Sit down and have some tea, Maggie," she said. "Was it too, too awful?"

"Not at all," said Maggie in a thin, little voice. "My lord tells me I gave a most creditable performance."

"Peter!"

"Well, she did," muttered the earl, kicking a log in the fire.

Miss Rochester's eyes flew from one to the other. "I wonder what the murderer will do when he reads the newspapers tomorrow," she said. "There's going to be a very worried man somewhere."

"Or woman," said the earl over his shoulder.

"Meaning me?" said Maggie, getting to her feet.

"This is all too much," remarked the earl

conversationally to the fireplace. "If the cap fits, by all means wear it."

"I can't believe this," said Maggie, eyes blazing. "You of all people to turn against me now. I think you're callow and horrible."

"Callow and horrible, am I?" said Lord Strathairn, mimicking her Scottish accent. "I think I have done a great deal for you. It's not everyone who would . . ."

"Give a murderess houseroom," said Maggie savagely.

"Peter!" said Miss Rochester. "You are behaving like a cad. Apologize to Maggie immediately."

The earl suddenly sat down at the table and gave Maggie a rueful smile.

"I'm sorry," he said, running his hands through his hair. "I'm tired and worried and I don't know what came over me. Please sit down, Maggie. I'm afraid my nerves are not as strong as I thought they were."

Maggie hesitated. He was smiling up at her, but the smile did not meet his eyes. All the fight went out of her and she sat slowly down again in her chair.

"Thank goodness that tiff's over," said Miss Rochester bracingly. "We'll never get anywhere sniping at each other. I must say, Maggie, it did my heart good to see you standing up for yourself. I don't think you've ever done such a thing before."

But Maggie was still too hurt to answer.

The earl looked at her bent head and suddenly felt sorry for her. He did not trust the strong sexual emotions she roused in him and ruefully admitted he was all too ready to believe the worst of her.

"I rather like Colonel Delaney," he said lightly, wishing now that Maggie could lose that stricken look. "But I think we've given him enough entertainment for one day. He'll probably leave with the Press."

But no sooner had the group of photographers and reporters made their way down the drive than the colonel erupted into the room, all set, it seemed, to continue eating breakfast.

The earl pulled his half hunter from his pocket and looked at it pointedly. "Wouldn't you like to stay to lunch?" he asked the colonel who had walked to the sideboard and was lifting the covers of various dishes.

"Very kind of you, old boy," said the colonel, apparently deaf to sarcasm, "but there's masses here and it's a pity to waste it, and we'll all need a good tuck-in before we go to Glasgow."

"Glasgow!" said three dismayed voices behind him.

"Of course!" The colonel's little shoe

button eyes were opened to their widest with surprise. "I've got to see young Robey and Ashton, and you've got to take Mrs. Macleod back to that home of hers in Park Terrace and ferret about and see what you can discover."

"I think Mrs. Macleod has had quite enough for one day," said the earl wrathfully, but to his extreme irritation, Maggie spoke up.

"I think I would like to go," she said. "I have more courage now. Miss Rochester and you, Colonel Delaney, have given me that courage." Maggie did not look at the earl. She went on, "Miss Rochester always has the knack of making even the worst situations seem quite ordinary."

"That's because she's a remarkable woman," said the colonel, smiling into Miss Rochester's eyes, and Miss Rochester gave a shy smile and privately vowed to wax her face again that very evening, no matter how much it hurt.

A gust of wind rattled the windows and howled in the chimney.

The earl was hurt — yes, hurt — that that ungrateful little cat, Maggie Macleod, had so pointedly left him out of her catalogue of the people who had given her courage.

It was downright indecent the emotions

kindled in him by the very sight of her pliant, curvaceous feminine figure. The hem of her skirt had caught on the chair and one delectable ankle was bared to his gaze. She was probably doing it deliberately.

All that breathless, meek innocence was a front. She was a siren who stole people's hearts as easily as she poisoned their tea.

He realized three pairs of eyes were fastened upon him. The colonel's eagerly, Miss Rochester's, puzzled, and Maggie's wide, unfathomable pools.

He shrugged.

"Glasgow it is," he said.

And then he felt himself shiver with a sudden, irrational feeling of doom.

Eight

Glasgow!

Although it was midsummer, great black clouds hurtled across the twisted chimneys of the city, sending slashing rain driving across the gleaming black cobbles and against the sodden walls of the black tenements. Even that famous shopping centre, Sauchiehall Street, looked bleak and forlorn, the flower sellers in their tartan shawls huddling in doorways, trying to protect their blooms from the force of the gale. One brave orange seller stood at the corner of Wellington Street, calling in a high, shrill voice, "Sweet Sevilles, and nane o' yer foreign rubbish."

"She probably thinks Seville is somewhere on the Clyde," muttered the earl as the carriage bearing himself, Miss Rochester and Maggie clattered along Sauchiehall Street towards Charing Cross.

The cross winds at Charing Cross made the carriage sway alarmingly. A square automobile chugged past at a dangerous twenty-five miles per hour.

From Charing Cross they began the winding climb up to Park Terrace, set on a ridge above the city.

Colonel Delaney had left them at the station to go in search of Lord Robey and Alistair Ashton.

A servant had been sent in advance to warn the housekeeper, Flora Meikle, of their arrival, and there she was, the same as ever, mouth perpetually drawn down in disapproval, her wrinkled hands clasped tightly in front of the black bombazine of her dress as she stood on the front step, the wind sending her black skirts swirling about her high buttoned boots.

"Welcome home, Mistress," she said with a tight grimace, which was all she could ever manage in the way of a smile.

The earl looked about him with interest.

The tall house was one-sided, that is, all the rooms led off on the right hand side of the hall and staircase.

Flora led the way upstairs to the drawing-room which was on the first floor, and then left them to go and fetch tea.

Maggie sat down at the table and looked about her. She felt she had grown much older in the past months. Another Maggie had sat here in the evenings, furtively watching her beefy husband, dreading the moment he would run his fat tongue over his fat lips and say, "It's time for your duties. Off to bed." He never described the sexual act as anything other than Maggie's duty. The new Maggie felt she would now have fought back, would not have allowed such bullying.

How terribly rich and grand and imposing Inspector Macleod's house had seemed to her naïve, unsophisticated eyes, and how dull and dowdy and old-fashioned it looked now.

The drawing-room was depressing to say the least. The mahogany furniture was massive. Sepia pictures of Highland moors and Highland cattle adorned the walls.

The room was dominated by a heavy square table, polished to a high shine and ornamented with one long plush runner down the middle on which stood, right in the centre, a large aspidistra in a brass bowl.

The housekeeper returned followed by the parlour-maid, Jessie, pushing a laden trolley.

First the plant and the runner had to be removed and the table covered with American cloth and then with a felt cloth, and then with a plush monstrosity with large bobbles round the hem, and then a lace cloth was finally placed on top of all that.

A massive silver teapot was carefully put

down on a special wooden stand and covered with a tea cosy of orange and pink wool. A huge four-tiered cake stand was placed on the floor beside them so that they had to stoop to reach the tiny cucumber sandwiches on the bottom plate.

Having seen to their needs, Flora Meikle dismissed the parlourmaid and then stood sentinel in the corner of the room.

"Oh, do go away," said Miss Rochester sharply, and, when the housekeeper had left the room, she added, "What a terrifying woman. Just like a wardress!"

"I would like to get started right away," said the earl. "I don't care if the grim housekeeper is hurt because we don't eat her beastly tea. Where's the inspector's study, Maggie? Or where did he keep his papers?"

"Downstairs at the back," said Maggie. "I think I would like to go to my bedroom and see if there are some things I could take with me. Not clothes, but books and pictures."

"Very well," said the earl. "Take Miss Rochester with you and leave me to Mr. Macleod's papers." He smiled at Maggie, but it was a mechanical, preoccupied smile.

"Did he really kiss me?" wondered Maggie as she led Miss Rochester up to the second floor. "Perhaps he was drunk. Men are strange when they are drunk. Goodness, he agreed to *marry* me when he was drunk."

A bit of the black day outside seemed to move into her heart.

She felt herself becoming angry with him. She wanted to be rude to him, shout at him, punch him, do anything to get a response.

The earl toiled away for an hour, going through a mass of papers which all seemed to be receipts, dating back some thirty years. The inspector had never thrown anything away, it seemed.

The door opened and Colonel Delaney came in, saying he hadn't seen either Ashton or Robey but the young men were expected at The Club for dinner at seven that evening.

"Find anything?" he asked, putting a hand on the earl's shoulder in what the earl considered was an overly familiar manner.

"There's nothing here," said the earl testily, moving his shoulder impatiently under the colonel's hand. "Only this scribbling on the side of the blotter. *Salamanca Street, Govan,* written over and over again."

"Well, we'd better go there and poke around," said the colonel.

The door opened and Miss Rochester erupted into the room, her eyes bulging. "You'd better come upstairs!" she screamed. "You'll never guess what we found."

Both men raced up the stairs to Maggie's bedroom. Maggie was sitting staring at an open jewel box. Diamonds and rubies and emeralds flickered in the gaslight, for the day was so dark the gas had had to be lit.

"Where did all that come from?" demanded the earl.

"I don't know," wailed Maggie. "It wasn't here before. I didn't own any jewellery at all."

Colonel Delaney rang the bell beside the fireplace and they all waited, staring mesmerized at the jewels until Flora Meikle walked into the room.

Maggie twisted around on the dressing-table stool. "What are these doing here?" she asked the housekeeper. "I've never seen them before."

"Well, I thought they must be yours, Mistress," said the housekeeper righteously. "After the trial I was redding up the cellar and I found this tin box in a corner behind the boiler. I thought you must have hid it there for safekeeping and when I got a message from my lord, saying as how you were coming today, I dusted it and opened it and found the jewel box inside and put it on your dressing-table."

"But I've *never* had any jewellery!" exclaimed Maggie.

Flora Meikle sniffed. "How was I to know? Mr. Macleod was aye saying as how you were the daughter of some rich laird."

"But it came out in court that I am a shop-keeper's daughter."

"Oh, aye," said Flora undaunted. "But there's a lot o' rich shopkeepers around. Just look at Mr. Lipton."

"Send for the police," said the earl, appearing to come out of a dream.

"And while you're at it, get the newspapers here as well. I want no cover-up just because Macleod was a policeman."

"What!" screeched Flora, shocked to the very core. "Are you trying to tell me that the maister was up to no good? That man was a saint, a veritable saint. 'No good will come o' marrying a young wife, and one o' thae Highland folk at that', that's what I told him."

"Damn your impertinence," said the earl wrathfully. "Send someone to fetch the police immediately. I don't suppose this dreary dump possesses a telephone."

"Well, that's where you're wrong, my lord," snapped Flora. "We mayn't be English, but Glasgow is the most modern city . . ."

"Oh, for heaven's sake," interrupted the colonel. "Where is the instrument? You stay here, Lord Strathairn, and you too, ladies. I won't be long. Come along, Miss Meikle. You should know not to bite the hand that feeds you. If Mrs. Macleod keeps you in her employ after that last outburst, then she's much more forgiving than I would be."

A bare half-hour later Maggie's bedroom was in an uproar.

The Press were back in force, waiting with bated breath while Superintendent John Menzies studied the jewels one by one and consulted a list handed to him by one of his subordinates.

He gave a heavy sigh. "Get the fingerprint kit up here," he said. "These jewels are all stolen goods."

"Are you trying to say that Inspector Macleod was a resetter?" asked one reporter, licking his lips.

"What does he mean by 'resetter'? muttered the earl to Colonel Delaney. "Do these idiots think the inspector reset stones as a hobby?"

"No," smiled the colonel. "This gets more and more fascinating. In Scotland, a resetter is what you would call in England a receiver, or in common slang, a fence. I wondered how the good inspector could afford a mansion like this."

"I'll no be saying a word right now," the

superintendent was saying severely to the reporter, "and I'll thank you to remember that."

"The Press can wait downstairs," said the colonel. "I'm sure they're dying to know the outcome."

But the gentlemen of the Press refused to budge. It was not often they had a chance to watch the fingerprint experts at work. Soon two men from the C.I.D. added their presence to the already crowded room and got to work, spraying white dust over the jewel box. Flora Meikle was sent to fetch the tin box in which the jewel box had been concealed and to find any personal articles of the inspector's which might still carry his fingerprints.

Colonel Delaney was explaining to Miss Rochester that he made a hobby of criminology and that this method of detection was called the Galton method, pioneered by Sir Francis Galton not so long ago.

At long last the detectives reluctantly gave their findings. Fingerprints on the tin box which had contained the jewels were those of Flora Meikle and Inspector Macleod.

"Aye, well," said Superintendent Menzies desperately, "Poor Macleod had probably taken them from a resetter and was on the point of putting in a report and handing them over when he was poisoned."

"But I'm afraid there's clear evidence the inspector hid the box behind the boiler," said one of the detectives. "There's clear marks of the inspector's hands, showing where he leaned on the boiler when he was trying to hide the box."

One reporter, overcome by hard work, a long day, whisky and excess of emotion was crying quietly in a corner. He still couldn't believe his luck.

"This is a black day for the polis, that it is," said the superintendent, relapsing into the vernacular in his shock.

"Didn't you ever think it strange that a police inspector could afford a house like this and servants on his salary?" asked the colonel curiously.

"Och, no," said Superintendent Menzies heavily. "He aye put it about that he had come into money after the death of his first wife and that his second had a powerful dowry. We saw no reason to doubt his word."

Maggie felt a strange sensation of elation and relief. Her husband had been a criminal. Therefore it followed that all men were not as her husband. She remembered how she had accepted his coarseness and brutality as normal behaviour. Now all those people who had testified that Inspector Macleod had been a fine upstanding man, a pillar of society, would have to think again.

The earl, Miss Rochester and Maggie sat down to dinner in the Central Hotel in Glasgow that evening in a more optimistic frame of mind. Miss Rochester was positively girlish and kept taking out a small mirror and studying her reflection and pushing wisps of hair back from her broad forehead.

"So," said the earl at the end of the meal, "I have decided that your late husband, Maggie, was an out-and-out villain, and some criminal considered he hadn't been paid enough for his loot and put arsenic in Macleod's tea."

"I would like to think that," said Maggie slowly, "but surely any criminal would hit my husband in a fit of rage or threaten to expose him. If my *husband* had murdered someone, then it might make more sense. I cannot see a criminal, a burglar, resorting to poison and paying some woman who looks like me to buy arsenic. I can't see any woman a criminal would employ being able to afford a coat with a sable collar. Och, the whole thing's daft."

"Good heavens, girl," snapped the earl.

"Here I am, doing my best to unravel this mystery and all you can do is raise stupid objections."

"They are not stupid," Maggie flashed back. "I knew my husband . . ."

"Oh, I see, you knew he was a criminal. Perhaps you are a criminal yourself."

"Peter!" Miss Rochester flapped her hands in embarrassment.

"I'm sorry," said the earl, not sounding sorry in the least.

"Let me go on trying to work this thing out. There's that thing he was working on with Knight. He was sure it would earn him the rank of superintendent. Surely it couldn't be anything criminal. It sounds more as if he were on the point of exposing someone. And it couldn't be any ordinary criminal because he would be expected to do that as part of his day's work anyway."

"Oh, here's the colonel!" cried Miss Rochester, turning red. "He will tell us what to think."

"I'm sure he will," said the earl dryly.

But the colonel was in a subdued mood and sat quietly drinking brandy while three voices tried to tell him all the possible explanations of the inspector's death.

At last he raised troubled eyes to the earl and said, "This is more than a simple piece of villainy. A lot of time and planning and money went into this murder. I saw Lord Robey and Mr. Ashton at dinner and they told me quite a shocking story after having extracted my promise that I would not go to the police."

Colonel Delaney briefly outlined Lord Robey's story of the marked cards and the bottle of laudanum.

"Why?" said the earl, looking dazed. "Why should Handley go to such lengths to humiliate me?" Maggie winced at the "humiliate".

"Well, Robey says Handley has a passion for revenge."

"That still doesn't explain it. He had never met me before. I did not say anything at all that could possibly have annoyed him. There was a prostitute with a baby tried to solicit him and he got rid of her very cruelly and I was angry. But that would surely not be enough . . ."

Miss Rochester clapped her hands. "But don't you see? *Handley* must be the murderer. He has a lot of money and by all accounts he's a thoroughly nasty man!"

"I thought of that," said Colonel Delaney quietly. "If Handley and the inspector met, then nobody ever saw them. Handley had no need to sell stolen jewels. It just doesn't make sense."

"I don't care what Robey says," said the earl grimly. "I'm going to sue Handley for the dirty trick he played on me."

The colonel fingered his moustache. "If you take Handley to court, Handley will revenge himself on Robey and Ashton by exposing their visits to a certain — forgive me, ladies —house of pleasure run by a Madame Dupont. Not only that, but the whole story of that marriage of yours would be made public. Do you want that?"

"Good gracious! *No!*" said the earl, looking appalled. Maggie flushed miserably and stared into her empty coffee cup but the earl did not notice.

"First of all, I think we should put up here for the night," said Colonel Delaney. "I took the liberty of telephoning Strathairn Castle and asking your man to travel up with a change of clothes for you all . . ."

"That's damned high-handed of you," stormed the earl. "You take too much upon yourself."

"I do, don't I," said the colonel. "But admit! What would you have done without me today?"

The earl looked at him stonily and then his handsome face broke into a reluctant smile.

"Do you usually take people's lives over like this?" he asked.

"Not usually," said the colonel. "Not since I was in the Greys when it was my job to order men around. But this is a bit like a battle, wouldn't you say?"

The earl threw up his hands. "It's a battle, Colonel. Let's hope we do not end up having a battle with you! What horrible plans have you for tomorrow?"

"I think we should investigate that Salamanca Street in Govan. We'll need to take the ladies with us, or Mrs. Macleod rather . . ."

"It doesn't sound a very salubrious address," protested the earl. "They would be better to wait here for us."

"No. I think they should come. Mrs. Macleod might recognize someone or something. Something that she's seen or heard and has forgotten."

"Very well," sighed the earl. "Oh, how I wish I were out of this confounded mess."

Miss Rochester was gazing adoringly into Colonel Delaney's eyes, the earl was yawning, and so no one saw the look of naked hurt on Maggie Macleod's face.

It was Roshie who prevented the ladies from going to Salamanca Street. He arrived at breakfast the next morning with a sheaf of newspapers.

The earl was slightly embarrassed at the enthusiasm and sentimentality of the stories. Maggie was portrayed as a model of Scottish womanhood and innocence who had been harshly treated by an inept police force, and the earl as a sort of Sir Galahad, riding to her rescue.

The full story of the inspector's jewels took up the inside pages. Reference was also made to the loyalty of the Strathairn servants, Mr. Roshie Munro being quoted as saying he had always known Mrs. Macleod had not done it and he was supporting his master in every way. Which was a lie. Roshie was still suspicious of Maggie. But he had been a gentleman's gentleman for years and could recognize a change in fashion or public opinion just before it happened.

When he heard of the proposed visit to Salamanca Street he said firmly it was "no place for a woman", and to Maggie's disappointment, the colonel and the earl elected to leave her behind with Miss Rochester.

She retired to her room, wondering how to pass the day. There was a knock at the door, and, thinking it was a hotel servant, she called, "Come in."

The earl stepped into the room. He stood just inside the door, looking at her.

Maggie was wearing a midnight-blue

215

silk velvet dress with a white spot pattern and white lace decoration. The sophisticated cut emphasized the roundness of her bosom, the tiny span of her waist and the soft well of her hips. Her eyes looked enormous in her pale face and against the black masses of her hair.

"Just popped in to say goodbye," said the earl, wondering what there was about Maggie that made him behave in such a stilted, unnatural fashion.

He was standing just inside the door. She rose and came to meet him.

"You will be careful," he said, taking both her hands in his.

Maggie could feel a tingling up her arms and tightened her grip in his. He looked down into her eyes and drew her gently towards him. Her lips were pink and beautifully curved. He noticed once again the beauty of her mouth.

He bent his head and Maggie closed her eyes.

"Lord Strathairn!"

The colonel's voice sounded from the corridor outside.

The earl muttered something under his breath and released Maggie's hands.

"Goodbye," he said awkwardly. "We shouldn't be too long."

"Goodbye," echoed Maggie faintly, letting her arms fall to her side.

He turned on his heel and was gone.

Maggie crossed to the window and stood looking out at the marching sea of umbrellas below her on Gordon Street. The wind had died down but rain was still falling steadily from a lowering sky.

"Oh, how I wish I were out of this confounded mess," he had said. If her name was cleared, what would her future life be like? Maggie wondered. Perhaps she would never see Peter, Lord Strathairn again. But he would not drop her entirely. That was not his way. He would ask kindly after her from time to time. He might even invite her to his wedding.

Better just to go away somewhere and try not to think of him again, try to forget a pair of warm lips against her neck and the way her body had ached and burned.

Dolly Murray read the newspapers in a stunned silence. The London newspapers did not usually concern themselves with what went on in Scotland, but a murder was a murder and an earl was an earl.

The stories they had printed were those that had been telephoned down to them by their Scottish colleagues. The photographs of Peter and Maggie had turned out very well and had arrived in time to catch the afternoon papers.

Picking up a gold fountain pen, Dolly carefully drew a moustache and a beard on Maggie's face and felt better. She realized with alarm that she had missed Peter terribly. She had been so quick to disassociate herself from him when it appeared he was socially ruined. But now he was being hailed as a knight in shining armour.

An image of the Strathairn fortune and the handsome Strathairn earl loomed large in Dolly's mind. August was approaching, and quite a lot of society took themselves off to the grouse moors and stately homes of Scotland. She racked her brain for some way in which she could secure an invitation to a home near Peter. Of course, she could just arrive at Strathairn Castle.

He could hardly throw her out. The more she turned over this last idea, the better it seemed. She would need to pretend to be sympathetic to that awful Scotch thing everyone was making such a fuss about. Dolly remembered the lovelight in Peter's eyes in their happier days. No, he was not indifferent to her. Far from it. It should be easy for a sophisticated woman of the world like herself to get him back on a string. The daughter of a Highland counter-jumper was no competition . . . no competition at all.

The Marquess of Handley threw down the papers. Why on earth had they not just hanged that tiresome girl and been done with it? He regretted that marriage business and hoped it would never come out. But he had had a longing to take that priggish earl down a peg or two. Crashing into the Scottish aristocracy and preaching morality, and he only an army captain and an Indian army captain at that.

It was time to call on Robey and Ashton and threaten them into silence again. There was no knowing what those two weak young men might do under pressure . . .

Salamanca Street seemed to crouch at the foot of a jumble of cranes and shipbuilding yards. It was one long row of black and evil-smelling tenements. The earl thought he had seen the worst of the poverty that Glasgow had to offer, but Salamanca Street proved him wrong.

Dirty children covered in scabs played barefoot in the rain. Huge shapeless women, their feet thrust into carpet slippers, shuffled along with their eyes on the ground. The men were small, stooped and almost all drunk. One lurched past, his red eyes focusing mindlessly on the earl and the colonel. "We arra people," he said, and the earl wondered whether it were a cry from the heart to tell these well-dressed strangers that they were still on the planet earth. The colonel thought it all sounded vaguely Bolshevist. The smell emanating from the closes was terrible. All about the air resounded with the hammer and clang of the shipyards, dreary, metallic, erratic sounds punctuating the dreariness of the scene.

A rag and bone man at the corner was exchanging filthy rags for even filthier ones, his pony shivering and stamping in the mud.

"Well," said the colonel with rather forced jollity, perhaps if we find out who owns this dreadful property, we might find a connection with the inspector. Let's try this first close."

Both men went up it a little way and then reeled out into the street, their handkerchiefs to their faces. "We'll need to try another one," gasped the earl. The close, or communal entrance, they had just tried boasted a broken stair lavatory with the door missing, and the contents had flooded down the stairs. "And did you see that creature holding a bottle of milk up to the gas jet?" said the earl. "What on earth was she doing?"

"Getting a cheap drunk," said the colonel. "When they can't afford anything to drink, they run the coal gas from the gas bracket through their bottle of morning milk as a substitute."

"Dear God," shuddered the earl. "I've a good mind to buy this property myself. Surely if these people were better housed, they might have a chance of leading normal lives."

"Oh, some of 'em would," said the colonel dryly, "the ones that don't gamble or drink. Buy it by all means, but don't expect a mass recovery. The evils of poverty burn deep. The children might benefit and that should be an incentive."

"Look, number four does not seem so bad as the others. Let us try it," said the earl.

The close to number four was smelly but free of refuse. They knocked at the first door and got no reply; the same at the doors of the first landing. On the second landing, there were four chipped, gashed and battered doors with the names of the occupants scrawled in pencil on the filthy whitewashed wall at the side.

The earl was beginning to wonder if they were going to find anyone at home, when, on the third try, the door opened and a little old lady peered out at them.

"We want to know who owns this property, Madam," said the colonel.

She stared at them for a long time and then jerked her head. "Come ben the hoose," she said, turning and walking back into her flat.

The earl and the colonel removed their hats and followed her into one room which served as kitchen, living-room and bedroom.

It was painfully bare, but clean. A box bed with thread-bare hangings took up one wall and a black coal range took up the other. There was one table and one chair, and, apart from that, the room had no other furniture.

"Why dae ye want tae know who owns the street?" asked the old lady, sitting down on the one chair and placing her red and wrinkled hands on the oilcloth covering of the table.

"I would like to buy it," said the earl.

Her faded blue eyes twinkled with amusement. "Buy Salamanca Street! Are ye wan o' thae rantin' Wullies?"

"No," said the colonel, seeing that the earl did not know what she was talking about. "My friend is neither a preacher nor a reformer. Why won't you just tell us who owns it?"

"Because I dinnae ken," she replied with some asperity. "We pay the rent tae the factors, Berry and Berry, in Hope Street. Of course, there's some that don't have tae pay, but I'm no wan o' them."

"Surely the owner cannot be a very bad fellow if he at least allows some of these miserable creatures to live rent free," said the earl in an aside to Colonel Delaney.

But the old lady's sharp ears picked up the aside and she gave a harsh laugh. "The wans that dinnae pay hiv got pretty lassies in the family. That's why."

"I don't understand," said the colonel. "Why should having a pretty girl in the family exclude one from paying the rent?"

The old lady rose to her feet, looking frightened, and started to push them towards the door.

"Ah've said too much," she kept muttering over and over again.

"But, dear lady," pleaded the colonel. "You have nothing to fear. We will protect you."

She opened the door and pushed them out onto the landing. "Off wi' ye," she said in a trembling voice. "Ye'll bring nothing but trouble."

The chipped door slammed in their startled faces. Out they went into the dismal street again, out into the dismal rain and the sights and smells and sounds of poverty.

"We'll try the factor," said the earl. "I gather that's what they call an agent here."

"We can if you like," said the colonel gloomily. "But I have a feeling we won't get much further."

At the factor's office, their demand for the owner of Salamanca Street was first met by dumb insolence and then, as they grew more insistent, with outright threats. They were finally told in broad vernacular just where to go and when they got there, to perform an impossible anatomical feat.

"Which leaves us exactly where we were," said the earl gloomily as they stood in Hope Street outside the offices of Berry and Berry.

"Not quite," frowned Colonel Delaney. "What was that business about young girls? Does the owner demand his *droit de seigneur?* I wish now we had stayed in Salamanca Street and tried some of the other tenants."

"Let's go into a pub and have lunch," said the earl. "I can't think on an empty stomach."

Over lunch of ashet pies and peas and beer, the earl and Colonel Delaney picked over the little information they had.

"You know," said the earl slowly, "all this

time we've been forgetting about the Marquess of Handley. What was that threat he made to Robey and Ashton to keep them quiet?"

"That he would report their visits to a brothel in Renfield Street to their families. A Madame Dupont runs the place."

"Strange," murmured the earl, and fell silent.

"The newspapers," he said at last. "Couldn't they help us to find the owner of Salamanca Street?"

"I doubt it," replied the colonel. "These factors are paid well to keep the names of the owner quiet."

"Well, if it isn't Captain Peter — Lord Strathairn!" The earl looked up and flushed guiltily as he saw his old friend, Mr. Farquharson, looking down at him.

"Sit yerself down," said the elderly tea merchant as the earl tried to rise to his feet.

He eased himself down onto the wooden settle next to the earl who introduced him to the colonel.

"There's no need to look so guilty," said Mr. Farquharson. "After reading about you in today's papers, I'm not surprised you didn't have time to call."

Now, Colonel Delaney was an enthusiastic amateur detective and he could not hear any conversation which took any interest away from the fascinating problem of who killed Inspector Macleod and so he promptly set about roping in Mr. Farquharson to help. He did not, however, tell him about the earl's 'marriage' to Maggie.

Mr. Farquharson listened in amazement to the long tale of intrigue and speculation.

"I think," said Mr. Farquharson at last, getting to his feet, "that I could easily find out who owns Salamanca Street. I have some useful contacts. You wait here a wee bit and I'll be back."

And so the earl and the colonel waited, each absorbed in his own thoughts.

After some time, Mr. Farquharson returned, flushed with success.

"Here's your man," he said, pushing a slip of paper across the table.

Colonel Delaney and the earl looked down at the name which seemed to leap out of the page.

"The Marquess of Handley."

"And," went on Mr. Farquharson, "he owns that place of Madame Dupont's in Renfield Street."

"So," said the colonel with great satisfaction, "we must pay a call on this Madame Dupont. There's obviously some connection between the pretty girls of Salamanca

Street and that house of pleasure."

Unnoticed by the three men, a small, wizened clerk from the offices of Berry and Berry slid out of the booth behind them and made his way quietly out of the pub.

Nine

Miss Rochester and Maggie enlivened the long day by reading novels and watching the increasingly heavy downpour slashing against the windows.

Miss Rochester was just going to suggest ordering tea when a hotel servant announced the Marquess of Handley.

"Oh, *no*," cried Maggie. "He's the man who forced Peter to marry me." But the words were hardly out of her mouth when the Marquess himself strolled into the room.

"What do you want?" demanded Miss Rochester harshly.

Maggie had half risen, putting a trembling hand out to a chair back to support herself, turning away from the marquess as she did so.

"I am here to escort you to the Earl of Strathairn," grinned the marquess, taking off his silk top hat and flicking off raindrops from its shiny surface with one long finger. "He has accepted my humble apology and awaits you at my house."

Maggie swung around to face him. "I don't believe you," she said.

"Oh, I would if I were you," said the marquess with unimpaired good humour. "Together we have managed to find evidence which acquits you, Mrs. Macleod, of the murder of your husband."

"How do I know you are not lying?" demanded Maggie.

"Well, I thought you might not believe me," said the marquess, sinking into a chair and neatly crossing his ankles, "so I brought along a note from Colonel Delaney."

He handed a piece of paper to Miss Rochester. The message was brief. "Please go with Handley. Strathairn and I will be waiting for you. Your troubles are over. Delaney."

Miss Rochester stared at it doubtfully.

Surely a gentleman like the colonel would sign off with something like Your Obedient Servant.

But Maggie's face had turned pink with excitement. "Do let us go, Miss Rochester. Just think! An end to the mystery at last."

Miss Rochester studied the marquess closely and he returned her scrutiny with a limpid gaze. He certainly seemed harmless enough. Then neither she nor Maggie had seen the colonel's handwriting before.

"We'll take Roshie with us," said Miss Rochester.

"I saw the earl's manservant when I arrived," said the marquess, "and sent him on ahead. I am sorry if you consider it a liberty."

Miss Rochester studied him in silence and the marquess spread out his hands in a rueful gesture. "I know what you are thinking, dear lady. There sits the man who coerced my nephew into a form of marriage with Mrs. Macleod. Very well, I admit my bad behaviour. To make amends, I set myself out to discover the identity of the murderer. That is why Lord Strathairn has forgiven me so freely."

"Who *is* the murderer?" asked Maggie.

"That is for Lord Strathairn to tell you. He felt it would come as a bit of a shock and he, understandably, does not consider me the right sort of person to break the news."

"We'll come with you," said Maggie suddenly. She did not know that her one burning motive was to see the earl again, to hear his voice, and to hope that he might look at her in that warm, intimate way he had once done when they had walked at midnight through the London streets.

Miss Rochester sighed and put her feeling of foreboding down to the grim weather.

Soon she and Maggie were hatted and booted and following the marquess out to his carriage.

"Where do you live, my lord?" asked Miss Rochester.

"Some little way outside the city," he replied. "It will not take us long to get there."

The journey took about an hour. Both women tried from time to time to elicit further information from the marquess, but he would only smile and say that he had promised the earl not to tell them anything, for the earl wanted to tell them everything himself.

The carriage stopped at last in front of a pair of imposing wrought-iron gates, waited while the driver jumped down and opened them, and then lurched up a short drive.

Miss Rochester and Maggie had only a faint impression of the outside of the house, for the rain was now being driven before a steadily rising wind, and the light, such as it was, was fading.

The marquess ushered them into a large, cold drawing-room.

"Our friends are obviously not here yet," he said cheerfully. "I'll get some tea and light the fire and you can make yourselves comfortable until they arrive.

Both women took off their wet mantles,

for they had been soaked in the short walk from the carriage to the house. The marquess made them a sketchy bow and left the room.

Maggie folded her arms about her shivering body, feeling a little twinge of dread. Why had they come so far, so readily, despite the colonel's note, with a man who had proved himself to be cruel and malicious to say the least?

The room smelled of damp and dry rot. There was no gas and it was lit by the light of a few candles. Glass cases full of stuffed animals lined the walls, the candlelight winking strangely in their green eyes until it seemed as if so many distorted Marquesses of Handley were crouched about the room, ready to spring.

The wind outside rose higher, a gust bringing on it the sound of children laughing and playing, a nostalgically normal sound to Maggie who began to feel she had left the real world behind such a very long time ago.

The door opened and a servant came in with a basket of logs. Both women watched in silence as he stooped to light the fire. He was a burly, ill-favoured fellow, more like an ex-prize fighter than a footman.

Having finished with the fire, he left and returned shortly with a tray of tea and biscuits which he set on a low marquetry table, urging them to "help themselves".

"Where is your master?" demanded Miss Rochester sharply, but the footman only shrugged his beefy shoulders in their tight livery and shambled from the room.

"I don't like this," whispered Maggie. "Oh, I wish Peter would arrive."

"Do you think the tea is drugged?" Miss Rochester picked up the teapot and stared at it, as if she could divine its contents from the outside. "I mean, they tried to get rid of Sexton Blake once, just like this."

Maggie smiled. "Oh, *boys'* stories."

"They're very good," protested Miss Rochester. "I mean, I think Sexton Blake is a far better detective than Sherlock Holmes." A dreamy look came into her eyes. "I see Sexton Blake as looking something like a younger version of Colonel Delaney."

"Well, I don't think the tea is drugged," laughed Maggie. "I mean, it's not as if we're prisoners. We can leave any time we like."

Both women smiled reassuringly at each other. Both were determined to believe that everything was normal and that the earl and the colonel would soon arrive, denying the evidence of their eyes and senses that everything was very far from normal.

No matter which stratum of society they

hail from, most people are prepared to think the best of anyone with a title. Plain Mr. MacTavish of the Gorbals, say, might be capable of dire plots, poisoning and murder. But not the Marquess of Handley. He had played a nasty trick on the earl, but then it was an age in which society specialized in playing quite horrific practical jokes on each other. One group of young men had recently pretended to be white slavers and had abducted one poor debutante, getting as far as carrying her bound and gagged aboard a yacht. The fact that she went into a delirium of fear did not really trouble the participants. It just went to show, they said, that some people couldn't take a joke.

And so Maggie and Miss Rochester, by mutual consent, returned to their chairs, prepared to take tea and cover their fears with social chit-chat.

And so they conversed about the weather while Miss Rochester poured tea.

Maggie was just raising her cup to her lips when Miss Rochester suddenly jumped to her feet.

"This is silly," she said. "I haven't the faintest idea where we are. I think it very odd that Handley should leave us alone so long. I'm going to find him and ask him what's happening."

Maggie put down her cup, untasted, and watched anxiously as Miss Rochester strode to the door.

Miss Rochester twisted and pulled at the handle of the door and then turned and faced Maggie, her heavy face almost ludicrous in its dismay.

"It's locked!" she said.

"It can't be." Maggie walked forwards and seized the door handle. Despite all her efforts, the door refused to budge.

Meanwhile, Miss Rochester had returned to the tea tray and had raised the lid of the teapot and was sniffing its contents, her heavy bulldog face wreathed in steam. "It smells funny," she whispered. "Come here and have a sniff at it, Maggie. Now, what does that smell remind you of?"

Maggie bent her head next to Miss Rochester's. "One of those laudanum mixtures," she said at last. "But it's too theatrical for words! Well, we won't drink it."

There was a silence while the wind roared about the house. "I think we should pretend to," said Miss Rochester in such a low voice that Maggie had to strain to hear her. "You see, if he thinks we're drugged, he won't tie us up or anything and we'll have a chance to escape."

"I'm scared," said Maggie. "I'm fright-

235

ened to death. Should we scream? We can't be very far away from anyone. I heard children playing not so long ago."

"The wind is very strong and carries sounds quite a distance," said Miss Rochester. "I don't think we're very near another house." She gave Maggie a quick hug. "See, we'll empty our cups out behind that curtain over in the corner, and then we'll lay ourselves down as if we've been overcome by the drug."

Too frightened now to argue or hope that they might be the victims of a practical joke, Maggie did as suggested. Miss Rochester sat down in her chair again and hung her head over the side. Maggie lay down on the hearthrug as if she had fallen over.

And then they waited.

Ages seemed to pass. Maggie felt her heart was beating so loudly that anyone entering the room would hear it. Her foot felt cramped and she eased it gently. Her nose tickled. What if she should sneeze?

At last there came the gentle sound of a key being turned cautiously in the lock.

Then the Marquess of Handley's voice, alarmingly brisk and loud. "Come here, Johnnie. They're out cold. You know what to do with them."

"Aye," came the gruff voice of the servant.

"I've tae take them doon tae the Broomielaw and gie them tae Captain Wheeler of the *Mary Jane*, bound for South America. He's tae pay me fur them. I winnae get much for the old 'un. They won't want anything as tough as that where she's goin'."

The marquess laughed rudely and said that in the part of South America to which the ladies were bound, the denizens would have intercourse with the house cat if there were nothing better around, and his servant gave a horrible guffaw while Miss Rochester burned with humiliation and rage.

"Put them in the cart," went on the marquess, "but cover them with a tarpaulin. I don't want the merchandise getting wet, let alone anyone seeing it. I'll wait here for Strathairn."

"Ye hate him, don't ye?" came the sly voice of the servant.

"He should never have meddled in my affairs," said the marquess in a conversational voice as if discussing the vagaries of the stock market. "I thought I had taught him a lesson once. He was preaching about the sordid property of Glasgow and saying piously that he was glad he didn't own any of it. The man has the soul of a counter-jumper. Now he's interfering. He's found out about Salamanca Street, and so, like

237

that fool Murdo Knight, he'll have to go. I paid that idiot of a reporter to keep his mouth shut but he got greedy. After you've got rid of these women, come back and tell me that all is well. I will then pay a call on Strathairn and tell him he must keep his mouth shut if he wants to see either of them again. That will give me a breathing space to think what to do about *him*."

Miss Rochester listened as hard as she could although the sound of her own heartbeats and the sound of the rising wind outside drowned most of the marquess's words. But she *had* heard him confess to murder. He had distinctly said he had killed Knight and he had surely indistinctly confessed to murdering Macleod. Surely he had said something about paying that idiot Macleod and Macleod getting too greedy?

Maggie felt dizzy and faint. It took all her small stock of courage to force herself to lie still and breath deeply and evenly. All they had to do, she thought, was wait until they were carried from the house and then try to escape.

All they had to do was 'play dead' and wait for the right moment.

Miss Rochester made an odd little sound, something between a cough and a sneeze.

"What have we here?" demanded the

marquess. He bent over Miss Rochester and thumbed open one eye. In vain did Miss Rochester try to roll it back in her head.

"Tie them up," snapped the Marquess. Maggie leapt to her feet and ran for the door. The servant brought back his fist and struck her neatly on the point of the chin and she went down like a stone.

"Maggie!" wailed Miss Rochester, struggling to her knees. She bent over the unconscious girl, helplessly rubbing her wrists. The Marquess nodded briefly to the servant who quickly took a thick little blackjack out of his pocket. One neat crack on the back of Miss Rochester's bent head and she slumped over Maggie's body.

"If they're clever enough to play games like that," said the marquess breathing rapidly, "then they may get up to some other mischief. Tie them firmly and gag them both. I had better come with you to the Broomielaw."

The servant, Johnnie, hesitated. "If Strathairn his foond oot about Salamanca Street, he'll go straight tae the police."

"Not he," shrugged the marquess. "He will need definite proof and that takes time. As soon as we've got these women on board, I'll call on him and tell him their safety depends on his silence."

Johnnie looked at his master, a worried frown creasing his low brow. The marquess's eyes were glittering with a hectic light and for the first time Johnnie began to wonder whether he was mad.

"Don't stand there glowering, man," snapped the marquess. "Move the bodies quickly. We'd better call at the Dupont woman's on the road."

The servant brought twine and began to tie the ankles and wrists of both women. Then he gagged them.

For the first time since he had started work for the Marquess of Handley did Johnnie experience a shudder of fear. Coercing slum girls into a brothel was one thing, but murder and kidnapping was another. He decided to make his escape from the marquess's employment that very day.

Colonel Delaney and Mr. Farquharson had decided that the earl should appear at Madame Dupont's in the guise of a client. They told him they would wait in the pub opposite, and, with that, they left him on the doorstep.

Madame Dupont looked the epitome of respectability in black silk, black mittens, and a small black hat. The earl wondered if he had made some terrible mistake. The entrance hall looked more like a dentist's waiting-room with its black marble fireplace and polished wood table and carefully arranged magazines.

"How can I help you?" asked Madame Dupont in accents that were more Fife than French.

The earl took the plunge. "I would like a young girl . . . er . . . as young as you can manage."

There was a silence while Madame Dupont studied him thoughtfully, her small eyes assessing the price of his clothes from his boots to the silk hat on his knee.

She touched a bell on the wall by the fireplace and a smart maid answered it, her apron crackling with starch. For one awful moment the earl fully expected to be shown the door.

"Annabelle," said Madame Dupont, "take this gentleman to Linda."

The maid gave a bob, and the earl, with a feeling of relief, rose to his feet and followed the maid out of the hall and up a flight of thickly carpeted stairs. On the second floor, the maid rapped at a door, pushed it open, and stood aside to let the earl pass.

The door closed softly behind him.

A very young girl, she could not have been more than sixteen, sat primly on a chair by

241

the bed. She was moderately pretty with a head of thick brown hair, but her expression was sullen and her mouth already seemed set in a perpetual pout.

She said not a word, simply stood up and reached for the fastenings of her dress.

"Don't," said the earl. "I mean, I just want to talk."

The girl, Linda, looked at him with sullen contempt. Obviously she considered him weird, and was mentally deciding to tell Madame Dupont to charge accordingly.

"Sit down," said the earl.

The girl sat down again and eyed him warily.

The earl drew a pile of sovereigns from his pocket and poured them from one hand to the other so that the gold flashed and glittered in the gaslight. Linda stared at the coins as if mesmerized.

"Ye must be wantin' something unco funny fur tae want tae pay in gold," she said, wrenching her gaze from the coins and looking thoughtfully at the poker as if wondering whether it would make a suitable weapon.

"No," said the earl, pulling up a chair and straddling it with his arms resting on the back. "I want some information. Tell me about the girls of Salamanca Street."

A flash of fear crossed the girl's face. "I ken naethin' about that," she said. "Tak' your money and go."

"Look here Linda . . . it is Linda, isn't it? . . . I shall not tell anyone anything you say. There is some connection between certain girls in this house and Salamanca Street, and I want to know what it is."

Once again his long fingers played with the gold.

"How mich is there?" demanded Linda harshly.

"Thirty gold sovereigns," said the earl softly. "Thirty. Enough to take you away from here, should you wish."

Linda ran a pale tongue over her dry lips. She rose and went to the door, and, opening it, looked out into the corridor. Then she closed it again and walked rapidly back to him, leaning against his shoulder and whispering urgently. "Gie me the money now. Let me feel it in ma hand tae gie me courage."

Hoping he was not being gulled, the earl put the money into both her small hands. She grasped the glittering coins firmly, and said, "Lean forwards. Lean closer tae me an ah'll tell ye."

The earl bent his head, and, stooping down, with one fistful of coins on his shoulder and the other fistful of coins buried in the folds of her dress, Linda began to speak in an urgent whisper.

"It's like this. My mammy couldnae pay the rent, and the man frae the factors comes around. He says tae Mammy he had work fur me up in the toon, and if I wad go wi' him, Mammy wouldnae have tae pay the rent again.

"Well, ah've two wee brithers and sisters and nae Daddy, and I knew whaur ah wus goin', fur there was always talk in Salamanca Street aboot whit happened tae the girls. Whit could ah dae? There wus that reporter, Murdo Knight. He cum aroon here wan nicht and questioned a girl called Jennie. She wus dragged frae the hoose that nicht and no one saw her again."

The earl's mind worked furiously. He must get the police and the Press. This place must be raided and all the girls lined up. He felt sure they would all talk to save their skins.

"Look, Linda," he said, "take the money and leave. This house is shortly going to be raided by the police and after that, no one will be able to touch you again. Do you think you can get away in, say, the next half-hour?"

Linda nodded dumbly, her eyes wide with terror.

"Go back to your mother's in Salamanca

Street," said the earl. "Wait there. Tell her that I will take care of her rent and that you can find decent employment."

Linda nodded again.

"Now what is the routine? Do I pay you?"

"No," whispered Linda, "unless I tell the auld bitch we've been up tae somethin' funny, ye pay the reg'lar price on your road out."

He let himself out quietly. Madame Dupont was waiting in the entrance hall as he settled his bill. She was extremely businesslike about the whole thing, he reflected wryly.

In no time at all he had joined the colonel and Mr. Farquharson and told them Linda's story. The men hailed a hansom and went straight to Central Police Headquarters to lay their evidence before Chief Superintendent Menzies.

To the earl's disappointment, the chief superintendent did not immediately order the Marquess of Handley's arrest. Mr. Menzies knew of several brothels in the city which were backed by wealthy men. Certainly, it did seem to suggest a reason for Macleod and Murdo Knight's murder. On the other hand, he did not want to bring the Marquess of Handley's wrath down on his head.

Mr. Menzies suggested they should raid

Madame Dupont's premises first and then go on from there.

The earl, Mr. Farquharson and Colonel Delaney waited in increasing impatience as the superintendent arranged a search warrant and then got his men together. Out they went into the windy, late afternoon.

The house in Renfield Street seemed strangely closed and quiet. A policeman seized the knocker and gave the door a resounding bang. An interested crowd began to gather.

"Break the door down," urged Colonel Delaney.

"We'll try a bit harder," said Mr. Menzies, turning up his coat collar against the biting wind. "Try again," he said to the policeman on the step. The policeman banged and banged on the knocker. They could hear the echoes resounding inside the house, resounding as if inside an empty house.

Mr. Menzies gave a massive shrug. "All right, boys," he said. "Break down the door."

A policeman came up with a large axe and smashed and hacked at the lock until with a cracking and splintering sound the lock gave and the door swung open.

The house was quiet and deserted. Even the magazines had gone.

"This is what comes of you taking so

much time over the matter," said the earl angrily to Mr. Menzies.

"We'll try the factors," said the superintendent.

With a rising feeling of frustration and anger, the earl went with the police to Hope Street. He already knew what they would find. The offices of Berry and Berry were as empty and deserted as Madame Dupont's house had been. Wooden filing cabinets stood empty, their drawers hanging crookedly open.

"We'll just need to go forward to the Marquess of Handley's residence," said Mr. Menzies ponderously. "He has a flat in the west end and a house on the outskirts of the city and a big mansion down in Ayrshire."

"Let's go, old chap," said the colonel to the earl. "I really think we should return and report to the ladies."

The earl opened his mouth to berate the superintendent and then closed it again. He felt immeasurably weary. He nodded and followed the colonel and Mr. Farquharson out of the factor's offices.

Mr. Farquharson said he was returning home, but that he would call on them in the morning. The earl and the colonel walked in moody silence towards the Central Hotel.

The earl suddenly saw Roshie standing on

the front steps of the hotel, desperately looking from left to right.

"Something's happened!" he said, breaking into a run.

"Oh, my lord," cried Roshie, his eyes bulging out of his head and his hands shaking, "the Marquess of Handley called at the hotel and told me you wanted me urgently at an address at Glasgow Green. But when I got there, I found there was no such address. Now the ladies have gone and I don't know where they are."

The earl brushed past him and ran into the hotel shouting for the manager. The staff was quickly assembled, questions asked. Soon it became all too clear that Maggie and Miss Rochester had left some time ago with a gentleman answering to the Marquess of Handley's description.

"The police will find them," said the colonel, although he looked worried to death.

"We can't just sit here," said the earl. "Damn these slow-witted policemen."

A small kitchen boy was shoved forward by the manager. "This lad has some information. Go ahead, Angus. Tell the gentlemen what you know."

The kitchen boy was a small white-faced individual with well-worn clothes covered by a spotless apron.

"I wus goin' off duty," said Angus, staring hard at his own shoes, "and I saw him come out with them two ladies and get in the carridge."

"We already know that," sighed Colonel Delaney, "but thank you all the same."

"Very well, Angus," said the manager, "you may go back to your duties."

Angus still stood staring at his own shoes. "Lovely horses they wus," he said. "Big an' black."

"Yes, *thank* you, Angus."

"Mad for horses I am," Angus told his shoes. "Hope he doesnae take them on the boat. It's blowin' up awfy hard down by the Broomielaw."

"What! What are you talking about?" demanded the earl.

"I was tryin' to tell you," said Angus plaintively. "I saw him first with the carridge and the two ladies when I was taking my break in the afternoon. Before I came back fur the evening, I went down to see my Ma. We live down near the Broomielaw. I saw the horses again. Down by the boats."

"Come along," said Colonel Delaney. "Please God we may be in time."

The hansom bearing the earl, the colonel, Roshie and the excited kitchen boy rolled onto the Broomielaw and stopped in front of a forest of tossing masts. The wind was howling and shrieking in the rigging.

"Now," said Colonel Delaney, startling the small party by pulling a serviceable-looking pistol from his overcoat pocket, "where did you see the carriage, Angus."

"It's still there!" said Angus, pointing down the quay.

They all set off at a run.

The carriage was empty, the horses tethered to a post tossing and bridling in the noise of the storm.

"He must be aboard that ship," said the earl. "Shout and see if you can rouse someone. The gangplank is up."

They all yelled but their voices were picked up by the wind and blown away in the opposite direction.

"I'm going to try to jump," said the earl, narrowing his eyes and trying to calculate the distance. "If I can make it, then I can lower the gangplank."

"It's very dangerous," said Colonel Delaney doubtfully. "If you miss, you could be crushed against the quay."

"I've got to try," said the earl, a picture of Maggie's pale, wistful face rising before his eyes.

He went back as far as he could from the boat, and then made a mad sprint and took off from the quay with a tremendous leap and landed with a crash on the deck.

"Quickly," called Colonel Delaney. "The gangplank."

The earl wrestled and fought with the large knots of the ropes which held the gangplank and at last succeeded on lowering it onto the quay. He was fretting at the delay, and yet knew he would probably need help if the crew turned out to be on board along with Handley.

As soon as the gangplank was secured, the earl did not wait for the others but began to search the ship. There was no sign of any crew. Since they obviously could not set sail in such a storm, they were probably all ashore. And yet the marquess's carriage was still there, so where was the marquess? Find him, and find Maggie, thought the earl.

He found Maggie and Miss Rochester in a forward cabin and he only found them by accident. The boat was plunging and reeling at anchor and he stumbled and sat down heavily on a berth and heard a stifled gasp. With trembling fingers he stood up and struck a match and lit the brass tilley lamp on the low ceiling. Then he turned back to the berth and ripped away a pile of old blankets and tarpaulins. Maggie's white face seemed to swim up at him like a body surfacing up from the water. He untied her gag and she gulped and gasped for air. "Peter," she whispered. "I thought he meant to suffocate us. I couldn't breathe."

"Where is he?"

Maggie looked bewildered and shook her head. "I was unconscious. I . . . I'm going to be sick. Oh, my head!"

"Miss Rochester. Where is she?"

Without waiting for an answer, the earl searched feverishly under the blankets on the opposite berth. Miss Rochester was revealed, her face a frighteningly purplish colour.

Colonel Delaney, Roshie and Angus came crowding into the cabin. "Angus," said the earl. "Untie the ladies. Colonel, bring that pistol and let's see if we can find Handley."

Out onto the deck they went again, out into the clamour of the storm. The marquess's carriage still stood on the quay.

"He's probably drinking with the crew in some pub nearby," said the colonel.

"You go and look," said the earl. "I feel he's still here. I'll go on looking. Take Roshie with you. As you say, he may have the crew with him."

The colonel and Roshie were half way down the gangplank when something made Roshie look around. The riding light on the ship next the *Mary Jane* swung in a wide arc and briefly illuminated a tall figure standing in the bow. It was the Marquess of Handley.

Colonel Delaney called to the earl, shouting as hard as he could against the noise of the wind. But the earl had already seen Handley.

The colonel and Roshie ran back on deck and unfastened the gangplank and let it fall down onto the quay. There should be no escape for the marquess that way.

The earl advanced on the marquess who watched his approach with great amusement.

"Good evening, Strathairn," said the Marquess of Handley pleasantly. "I am about to blow your brains out which will give me infinite pleasure."

Still smiling, he put his hand in his pocket, and then a baffled look of dismay crossed his face. He had left his pistol below in the cabin.

As the earl ran towards him, the marquess turned about and plunged over the side of the ship and straight down into the churning water. Without a second's thought, the earl dived after him. Peter, Lord Strathairn wanted revenge.

The Marquess of Handley was one of those swimmers who cannot bear to get their faces wet and so he swam a breaststroke, poking his head and shoulders as high above the water as he could. He turned to look over his shoulder. There was a terrific roar as a great gust of wind struck the *Mary Jane*. The ship swung out wildly at great speed and hit the Marquess of Handley's head with a sickening crack and he sank like a stone.

The earl who had dived when he saw the boat begin to swing, surfaced and looked about wildly. Then he dived where he had seen Handley go down and searched about in the roaring blackness with little hope of finding anything. But suddenly, just as he felt he could not hold his breath any longer, his fingers touched cloth. He grabbed hold of it and swam for the surface.

He brought the Marquess of Handley's body up with him. Roshie, who had been throwing every lifebelt on board desperately into the water, shrieked something about the police arriving. The earl swam round the plunging boat and urged the marquess towards a flight of stone steps cut into the wall of the quay. Hands reached down to help him as he thrust the marquess before him out of the water.

The earl ignored the reaching hands and turned Handley round. "Who killed Macleod?" he cried. "Did you kill Macleod?"

He shook the marquess roughly by the sodden shoulders of his coat.

The Marquess of Handley's head lolled to one side, his mouth set in a jeering grin.

His neck was broken.

Shivering and sick and weary, the earl let go his grip, dimly aware of shouting voices, bobbing lanterns and hands hauling the Marquess of Handley's dead body up onto the quay.

Then he became aware that Roshie had a strong arm about him and was helping him up the steps.

Johnnie, the Marquess of Handley's servant rounded the corner of a warehouse and saw the dark police uniforms and melted quietly back into the shadows. He was one witness the law would just have to do without.

Three hours later, the earl was comfortably wrapped in his dressing-gown and sharing a celebration bottle of brandy with Colonel Delaney.

He felt he had a great deal to celebrate. For Miss Rochester who proved to have quite amazing stamina had recovered sufficiently from her ordeal to give the police a full statement. She said she had distinctly heard the marquess tell his servant that he had killed both Macleod and Murdo Knight. The servant, Johnnie, had disappeared and a warrant was out for his arrest but everyone was relieved to have such a reliable witness in Miss Rochester.

Only Maggie, weak and shaken, had protested that the marquess had not admitted to murdering Mr. Macleod. But by the time she had heard Miss Rochester's version of the story for the third time, she became convinced that Miss Rochester had indeed heard everything and that her own fear had stopped her, Maggie, from hearing properly. After all, it couldn't have been anyone else.

Maggie had at last fallen asleep, fighting down a feeling of nausea from the blow on her head and a feeling of acute disappointment. After all, when the love of one's life rescues one from deadly peril, he should at least murmur some words of love, not rush off leaving one to the tender administrations of the kitchen boy!

Ten

Maggie and Miss Rochester sat in Maggie's private sitting-room at Strathairn Castle . . . and brooded. Maggie was in love with the earl but was sure her recent cold behaviour had chilled him off. Miss Rochester was in love with Colonel Delaney and had sadly come to the conclusion that her love would never be reciprocated.

The day outside was clear and warm. Three weeks had passed since the sensation of the Marquess of Handley's death. They were no longer a source of interest to the Press. Everything should have been perfect.

Maggie's business affairs had been competently handled by the earl's lawyers. The house in Park Terrace had been sold. Flora Meikle had accepted a pension, saying she intended to retire.

She invited the parlourmaid, Jessie, to accompany her, saying with a trace of grim humour that she had always wanted a servant of her own. She had taken a cottage outside

Largs on the Clyde coast, and Maggie was glad to see the last of her.

Both Maggie and Miss Rochester had been asked by the earl to stay at Strathairn Castle for as long as they liked. The warmth of his eyes as he had looked on Maggie had held an invitation to her to stay forever. But that had been before she had ruined the whole thing.

Maggie sighed, remembering that disastrous evening. It had been shortly after their return to the castle. Dinner had been a jolly affair with the colonel telling jokes and stories. Maggie had basked in the warmth of the earl's blue eyes. He had pressed her hand under the table and she had returned the pressure. Little tingles of anticipation had started to run up and down her spine. She knew he would take her in his arms, sometime before the evening was over, and that he would kiss her.

The very restrictions of polite society that were imposed on their behaviour had made passion between the two run high, while outwardly they both laughed at the colonel's jokes and teased Miss Rochester on the glory of her new scarlet silk gown.

At last the earl had turned to Maggie and had suggested a stroll in the garden.

With a fast beating heart, Maggie had

taken his arm and had walked with him into the sweet smelling night gardens. There was a large yellow moon above the cedar trees. The night was very calm and still. She loved him. Her heart was at peace. He was not as other men. He would not grab or paw or maul. He would take her in his arms and plant chaste kisses on her mouth, and he would ask her to marry him.

Maggie remembered her own lustful feelings when she had lain in his arms on the banks of the Crash.

She gave a little shudder of distaste. That had been the old Maggie. Now she was truly a lady, and ladies did not have such vulgar emotions. This passion she felt for him was something spiritual, something noble.

And then he stopped and pulled her roughly into his arms. He held her tightly pressed against the length of his body while he kissed her ferociously with all the fury of pent-up passion and longing, finally released.

Maggie had let out a choked sound of fear and wrenched herself free, wiping her hand across her mouth and staring at him in wide-eyed horror.

He did not love her; did not respect her. He would not treat her with such abandon if his intentions were honourable. He did not think her a lady and so he was treating her the way he would treat a woman of the streets.

He looked down at her in amazement. "Maggie," he had said, his voice wondering.

She had simply turned and run away.

And that had been that.

The following morning, the earl had been punctiliously chilly and polite. Maggie had desperately wanted to explain to him what had caused her fear — still wanted to explain to him — but modesty and bewilderment had kept her silent.

A week ago Dolly Murray had arrived with Hester in tow.

Instead of showing her the door, the earl had given her a curt welcome and had then plunged into the affairs of the estates. He had asked Colonel Delaney for his help and both men were out most of the day, in the fields or around the tenants' farms and cottages.

Dolly Murray had insidiously taken over the reins of the household, and neither Maggie nor Miss Rochester was experienced enough to remove them from her grasping hands.

Dolly had now begun to play hostess, asking various members of the county to dinner, and the earl seemed to find nothing amiss.

Miss Rochester was held back from her customary forthrightness of manner by her languishing love for Colonel Delaney. But at least she had not allowed Dolly Murray to take the head of the table. A small victory, but a victory for all that. Then it had gradually dawned on Maggie and Miss Rochester that their neighbours expected the earl to announce his engagement to the Merry Widow.

Miss Rochester's heart had begun by aching with sympathy for Maggie and then had ached with pity for herself. For Colonel Delaney had pronounced Dolly Murray to be "a rattling good sort".

Mrs. Murray's rippling laugh sounded from the garden, and the two women looked gloomily out of the open window.

Dolly Murray was presiding over the tea table which had been set on the terrace below. The earl was smiling at something she had said and Colonel Delaney was looking quite enchanted.

"It's no use," said Miss Rochester, voicing Maggie's thoughts. "I can't compete. She's years younger than I."

"Well, I'm younger than Dolly Murray," sighed Maggie, "but Peter never seems to see me now when she's around. Did she say anything about leaving?"

Miss Rochester shook her heavy head.

"She won't. Not till she's got a ring on her finger."

"I can't take much more of it," said Maggie suddenly. "I've watched and waited, hoping Peter would fall in love with me. But we're worlds apart socially. Dolly Murray makes me aware of that every time she opens her mouth. I'm not a lady. Perhaps that's why Peter . . . Oh, never mind. I've just got to get away. If Peter proposes to her, I don't want to be here."

"I can't stand the sight of her myself," mourned Miss Rochester. "Flirting and ogling with my Colonel Delaney."

"It's not as if I'm destitute," went on Maggie, thinking aloud. "I've got the money from the sale of the house and furniture as well as the money Mr. Macleod had in the bank. I'm surprised the court allowed me to keep it, considering most of it must have been from ill-gotten gains. I could get away. I could go back to Beauly and see what's happened to the shop. I've never heard a word from my father since I was accused of murder."

"And a good thing too," said Miss Rochester roundly. "Of all the unnatural parents . . ."

"But don't you see," said Maggie earnestly. "It would give me a purpose. A reason. I'm not afraid of my father anymore. To tell the truth, I feel like giving him a good piece of my mind."

"I'll go with you," said Miss Rochester, "if you'll let me have one more evening. Perhaps they don't find Mrs. Murray attractive and are only being polite. Perhaps our jealousy is making us read things into the situation that don't exist."

"Very well," said Maggie slowly. "Let's go and join them for tea. There's nothing we can do, sitting up here."

Maggie studied herself in the mirror. Normally she would have been pleased with her appearance. She was wearing a new pink organza gown with a high collar and a little white dot pattern, long tight sleeves, and a long skirt cunningly cut to mould itself over her hips. But everything she wore seemed to pale to dowdiness before Dolly's brash vitality.

She wondered whether she should confide in Miss Rochester and tell her of how she had repulsed Peter's advances, and why. But one did not talk about such things. Besides she had just confessed to Miss Rochester that she, Maggie, was not a lady and Miss Rochester had not protested. In her low state it did not dawn on Maggie that Miss Rochester might not have heard the remark.

Both of them went silently and gloomily downstairs and out onto the terrace.

"Oh, *there* you are!" cried Dolly gaily. "Where *have* you been?"

"Talking," said Miss Rochester grumpily.

"Oh, you old-fashioned misses do prefer the company of your own sex. Now, I am quite happy with the gentlemen."

"Particularly when they're generous," muttered Hester who was sitting alone at the end of the terrace, kicking a piece of moss out from between a crack in the paving with the point of one French shoe.

"And we are quite happy with you, ma'am," said the colonel gallantly. Miss Rochester stared moodily into the depths of her tea cup.

The earl leaned back in his chair and covertly studied Maggie Macleod's face. What was she thinking? Ever since the night she had repulsed him so rudely, he had battled with his hurt feelings and had kept out of her way as much as possible.

He had been furious when Dolly Murray had arrived on a visit without so much as a by-your-leave. Then after the initial shock had worn off, he wondered if he could perhaps make Maggie jealous.

But Maggie had simply become more silent and withdrawn. They had been playing croquet the day before and he had put an arm around her waist to show her how to hold the mallet and he had felt her physically shrink from him.

He did not know that Maggie had been alarmed at the vulgar emotions aroused in her body by his lightest touch.

There was a commotion inside the house and the sound of high girlish giggles and the Misses Bentley, followed by Mr. and Mrs. Farquharson, came into the garden.

The sisters were wearing pink and blue checked taffeta gowns, embellished with many frills and bows. They carried pink and blue checked parasols to match their dresses, pink and blue sun bonnets on their heads, and pink and blue dorothy bags dangling at the wrist.

In his unsophisticated way, Mr. Farquharson considered the Misses Bentley the flower of Scottish womanhood, and since he was also fond of their parents, had been hoping still to marry one of them off to the earl. Mr. Farquharson had seen no evidence of any warmth in the earl towards Mrs. Macleod and judged his intentions in that direction to be purely chivalrous.

The introductions having been made, Dolly launched into a fund of London gossip in the hope of keeping the earl's attention to herself. Hester, however, who had joined the group, interrupted her rudely with, "It's very bad manners, Auntie, to talk about people no one here has heard of."

Dolly bit her lip. By the time she had rallied, Morag Bentley was teasing out her shoulder ruffles and making little digging remarks to Maggie. Didn't Mrs. Macleod find it *strange,* after having been brought up in a shop, to live in a castle with all these servants?

Wasn't Mrs. Macleod so grateful to the earl for risking his reputation to save her? To all of this, Maggie answered "no" and "yes" very calmly, and after a few moments, begged to be allowed to retire. Miss Rochester went with her.

"I think the Bentley girls are the final straw," said Miss Rochester when they were alone. "I've been a very silly woman. Thinking I could attract a man at my age! But I didn't feel like the old me *at all* in all my new clothes. I'm awfully old."

"You're the same age as Colonel Delaney," said Maggie softly. "I thought he had a sparkle in his eye when he looked at you."

"I think it's pity," said Miss Rochester, "if you know what I mean."

"Oh, yes," said Maggie softly. "I know what you mean."

Downstairs, the earl was standing in the hall arguing with Colonel Delaney. "Look, you *can't* go!" he was protesting.

"Well, I feel I've got to, don't you know," said Colonel Delaney. "Trespassed on your hospitality long enough and all that."

"But to leave me with this gaggle of females for dinner."

"Thought you liked Mrs. Murray," mumbled the colonel.

"Not much."

"Don't look like that. Seems to me you've been deliberately ignoring Mrs. Macleod."

"No, you got it wrong, as the Americans say. *She's* been ignoring me. Tried to kiss her and she pushed me away as if I disgusted her. She feels a debt of gratitude to me and I don't want to take advantage of it again. What about you and Aunt Sarah?"

"Miss Rochester? Oh, splendid woman, salt of the earth and all that sort of thing, but nothing there, old boy. I'm a confirmed bachelor."

"Anyway, do stay for dinner," begged the earl. "I'll get rid of Mrs. Murray somehow, the Misses Bentley and the Farquharsons are only staying the evening, and then we can be comfortable again."

"Oh, very well," said the colonel reluctantly.

But as dinner wore on that evening, both the earl and the colonel became extremely restive, for there was no sign of Maggie and Miss Rochester.

At last, the earl summoned a footman and told him to find out what had happened to the ladies.

The footman seemed to be away for a long time. When he at last returned with a note in his hand, the earl almost snatched it from him.

It was from Miss Rochester. His aunt had only written a few lines. "Dear Peter, Maggie wishes to return to Inverness-shire to see if she can pick up her old life. She begs me to thank you for all you have done. She did not want to say goodbye since it would have been too painful . . . and too painful for me as well. My regards to Colonel Delaney. Yr. Loving Aunt, Sarah."

"When did they leave?" demanded the earl.

"Just after the dressing gong, my lord," said the footman. "Miss Rochester was most insistent that you were not to be disturbed."

"Oh, has that Mrs. Macleod gone?" laughed Dolly. "Really, these little shop girls have no manners. Breeding will out, I always say."

"Excuse me." The earl rose to his feet and

signalled to Colonel Delaney who followed him from the room.

"Well, well, well," said the colonel, rubbing his hands. "This is like old times. I do like a bit of action."

"What do you mean?"

"Why we're going after 'em, of course. Anyone can see you're in love with Mrs. Macleod. Now you are, aren't you?"

"Yes," said the earl with a sudden feeling of exhilaration. He realized he loved Maggie so much, why!, he could make her love him. "Yes, very much."

"And you'd better have me along because a little thing like Miss Rochester isn't fit to go gallivanting about the countryside without a man to help her."

The earl blinked at the idea of anyone describing his aunt as "a little thing". "What about my guests?" he demanded. "We can't just go off and leave them."

"Why not? *You* didn't invite them and with any luck by the time we return, Mrs. Murray will have taken herself off. Come along. We'll catch the night train."

The next day Maggie and Miss Rochester stood outside the door of Maggie's father's shop on the Beauly road.

"Well, he's not here," said Miss Rochester,

after rattling the door handle and banging on the glass.

"Is it Maggie Fraser?" asked a voice behind them.

Miss Andrews, the local schoolteacher, stood blinking myopically at Maggie and Miss Rochester.

"Oh, Miss Andrews," said Maggie. "I'm looking for my father."

"He's gone, and good riddance," said Miss Andrews. "He sold his stock and left for America. I have the key with me. The auld scoundrel asked me to check the shop from time to time to make sure no one had broken in. The one thing he didn't do was to sell the shop. Said he would come back to the place of his birth to retire. The man's mad, saving your presence Maggie . . . I mean Mistress Macleod," said the schoolteacher, taking in the finery of Maggie's clothes for the first time. "We read about you in all the papers. Quite a bit of excitement it caused. Anyway, as I was saying he's mad to talk about Beauly as his birthplace for it was established as a fact that he was born in Skye, and he just liked to say he was from the mainland because he thought that was a grander place, as if anyone cared."

As she was talking, the schoolteacher

turned the key in the lock and swung open the door.

Maggie breathed in the familiar cheesy, peppery, spicy smell of the store.

"Now is there any way I can help you?" asked Miss Andrews. "We were all a wee bittie conscience-stricken what with the way we all stood back and let your father marry you off to that terrible man."

Maggie smiled. "No, I just want to look around and see what I can do. I'll return the key to you when we have finished. We may stay the night in the Lovat Arms in Beauly."

"Come and have tea at the schoolhouse when you're ready," said Miss Andrews, "and you can tell me all about the trial. It was like a shilling shocker to read about your experiences in the newspapers."

Miss Rochester thought the last remark insensitive in the extreme, but Miss Andrews had taken her leave before she could think of a reply.

Maggie and Miss Rochester wandered aimlessly about the dusty shop after the schoolteacher left. They went upstairs and threw open all the windows, letting the sweet, fresh Highland air drift through the rooms.

Maggie leaned her elbows on the sill and

stared out over the Beauly Firth. "I shouldn't have come," she said in a low voice. "Too many ghosts here. Too many memories of beatings." She turned and faced Miss Rochester. "I had not known any kindness in my life, you see, until I met you and Peter."

Tears began to run down Miss Rochester's face. "It's all so hopeless," she sobbed, and Maggie knew what she meant. You cannot fall out of love just by running away.

"Shop!" cried a loud, imperative voice downstairs.

"Oh, dear," said Maggie. "We left the door open. I'll go down and get rid of whoever it is."

Maggie ran down the stairs and Miss Rochester slowly dried her eyes. She wished she had stayed in her safe, boring life at Beaton Maiden.

Well, at least she could offer to take Maggie back with her, and they could set up house together and grow old and unloved together, and the whole picture was so utterly miserable that Miss Rochester almost began to enjoy it in a horrible kind of way.

"Miss Rochester!"

She looked through her tears. Colonel Delaney was standing on the threshold. He gave an odd little duck of the head and went to stand beside her at the window.

"I've been thinking," he said, without looking at her, "that life's been very flat since the murder business. Been thinking about going to the South of France. Have a bit of a flutter at the tables."

"Oh," said Miss Rochester miserably.

The colonel took his walking-stick and began to draw patterns in the dust on the floor.

"Er . . . well, it's like this. Not much fun by myself. Wondered if you'd care to toddle along with me?"

Miss Rochester turned quite pale. "I mean," he went on anxiously, "Mrs. Macleod's being taken care of. Came with Strathairn, don't you know."

"Are you asking me to go to the South of France?" asked Miss Rochester in a queer, strangled voice, totally unlike her own.

"Yes."

Large bosom heaving, Miss Rochester clutched onto the window ledge to steady herself. That miserable little picture of herself and Maggie pining away in Beaton Malden fled from her mind.

She, Miss Sarah Rochester, was being propositioned for the first time in her life. The least she could do was cope with the situation like a lady.

"Thank you, Colonel Delaney," she said

politely. "I should like to go very much indeed."

The Earl of Strathairn and Maggie Macleod were walking along the shores of the Beauly Firth at least six feet apart.

Seagulls wheeled and cried mournfully overhead. The tide was out leaving an expanse of slimy rocks and brown seaweed.

He had suggested a walk to cover his awkwardness. Somehow, he had hoped the surprise of seeing him again would break down her reserve and that she would throw herself into his arms. But she seemed very calm, cool and chillingly polite.

"Maggie," he said, stopping and facing her. "Do you plan to stay here?"

She looked at him a long time. She seemed to be summoning up her courage to say something. At last, to his surprise, instead of answering his question, she blurted out, "Are ladies allowed to be passionate?"

"It sounds like a clue in a word game," said the earl. "What *do* you mean?" Maggie blushed and hung her head.

Then in a flash, he remembered his distrust of her. He remembered his old peculiar ideas that ladies did not go in for passionate lovemaking. He remembered most of the polite world professed to believe the same. So *that* was why she had repulsed him!

"Maggie," he said, choosing his words carefully, "passion knows no boundaries or class. Between a man and a woman in love, it is the most exhilarating, beautiful emotion."

A pale golden sunlight filtered through the grey clouds above and the gold of the sunlight seemed to flicker in the depths of Maggie's eyes as she looked at him.

"My name," she said slowly, "is not Maggie Macleod. I am Miss Margaret Dunglass, your cousin, and your friend."

He stumbled twice in his rush to take her in his arms, saying over and over again, "I love you. Marry me. I won't take no for an answer. I love you so much. Marry me."

Maggie raised her mouth to his, and he held her very close, kissing her and kissing her, kissing away all the murders and worries and doubts and fears.

"You are not Maggie Macleod," he said at last. "You are the Countess of Strathairn, and my wife."

"You can't want to marry me," said Maggie, but her eyes were shining with all the love in the world.

"We *are* married," laughed the earl. "But we'll be married in church as soon as possible. I see you don't believe me, so I am going to *make* you believe me if we have to stay here all night."

He bent his mouth to hers again, and they stayed locked in each other's arms for a very long time while the sun set behind the hills of the Black Isle and the incoming tide crept up around their feet.

When they finally made their dazed way back to the shop it was to find the colonel and Miss Rochester had gone. They stood looking at each other in the dim light of the store.

"Why didn't they wait?" asked Maggie.

"They probably saw us from the window and knew their company was superfluous," said the earl. "Too late for us to go any-where." Maggie held out her arms to him.

He swept her up in his arms and made for the stairs, leading to the bedrooms above.

"Peter," murmured Maggie against his ear. "You know, I swear the Marquess of Handley did not say anything about mur-dering Mr. Macleod."

"Mmmm," said the earl, his mouth against her hair. "Oh, he did it, mark my words. No one else had any reason to. Kiss me again, Maggie, my wife, and let's forget about the murder. Justice has been done. Now we've only got each other to worry about."

He laid her gently on the bed and began to unbutton the front of her dress.

Miss Flora Meikle looked around her spick and span cottage with a pleased eye. It was great to be able to retire with a good pension and have Jessie to look after her.

Jessie was a good girl and had never forgotten the day when Miss Meikle had taken her into service and rescued her from a life of prostitution. Since that day she had served the elderly housekeeper with a fierce devotion.

The door opened quietly and Jessie came in with the tea tray and set it down on a low table in front of the fire.

"You may join me, Jessie," said Miss Meikle grandly. "I feel like a bit of company."

Jessie sat herself down opposite Miss Meikle, eyes downcast, hands folded neatly in her lap.

"You're a good girl," said Miss Meikle. "Help yourself to tea. We've never really talked about it, you know."

Jessie nodded. She did not have to ask what "it" was.

Of course, it was a bit of luck you looking something like Mrs. Macleod and then these silly apothecaries couldnae tell sable from rabbit. You'll be able to wear that mantle and dress again, now all the silly fuss is over."

"I felt a wee bit bad about it," said Jessie, "especially when they arrested Mrs. Macleod, but I knew you wouldnae let her hang."

"Och, no," said Miss Meikle comfortably. "Mind you, I thought she would get hard labour, but that never did a body any harm."

Jessie raised her wide brown eyes and looked thoughtfully at her mistress. "I've never asked ye, mum, but why did ye poison auld Macleod?"

Miss Meikle sipped her tea reflectively. "Well, life is strange, Jessie. I got so's I couldnae stand the sight o' the man, him and his bullying ways.

"Up till the last minute, I didnae mean to do it. Mrs. Macleod didn't know I went into the study a few minutes after she took in his tea.

"I went to check the fire had enough coal. I'd been carrying the arsenic powder I told you to get me in the pocket of my apron. But it was like a talisman, something that made me feel strong, able to put up with him. An' to think I told them all I thocht he was a saint. Saint Lucifer, more like.

"Well, he was sittin' at the desk, grumbling away as usual an' he was holding the tea cup wi' those great red hands o' his with the black hairs on the back o' them. Fair gie'd me a scunner. He went to look out of the window, and I tipped the powder into his tea. I knew he always took two or three sips for a start and then he would tip the whole lot doon his craw. That's what he did.

"I whipped mysel' out o' the house and down tae the shops in Sauchiehall Street, talking to as many folks as I kenned so I could say as wisnae home at the time.

"Och, weel, there's some folk better off dead.

"Have a scone, Jessie. They're very good, yes, very good indeed . . ."

We hope you have enjoyed this Large Print book. Other Thorndike Press or Chivers Press Large Print books are available at your library or directly from the publishers.

For more information about current and upcoming titles, please call or write, without obligation, to:

Thorndike Press
295 Kennedy Memorial Drive
Waterville, Maine 04901 USA
Tel. (800) 223-1244

OR

Chivers Press Limited
Windsor Bridge Road
Bath BA2 3AX
England
Tel. (0225) 335336

All our Large Print titles are designed for easy reading, and all our books are made to last.